Beltane Bewitchment

Chapter One

Kinsley

"Where is it?" I found myself yelling much louder than I'd intended.

"Mom's yelling again," Laney called from down the hall where I hoped she was brushing her teeth. Like I'd asked her to do three times...

It wasn't like my Laney to disobey, but there was an electric current in the air. It was making us all a little weird.

She'd finally relented and stomped off down the hall with her little sister, Hekate, in tow. Hekate never listened. She was her own witch morning, noon, and twice at night. But other than her obsession with darkness and chaos magic, she was a super chill kid. I didn't have to tell her much, and therefore, she didn't defy me that often.

The knowledge that I was yelling again brought my husband, Thorn, to the bedroom door. He stood there stretched across the frame looking as handsome as the day I'd met him. Something about a six-foot man, with those biceps, poured into a uniform, really got my blood pumping. Even after all the years that we'd been married, his blue eyes could still make my stomach flip-flop.

But not that day. I needed to find that book. "I need to find the book!" I said when Thorn narrowed his gaze at me.

"I'd help you look, but I have to go," he said. "I'm so sorry."

"It's not your fault," I said and threw my hands up. "I still can't believe that mayor planned the grand opening for the new sheriff's station on the same day as the festival begins."

"He didn't believe the grand opening would get much attention if he didn't do with when all of these... tourists were in town," Thorn said with a chuckle.

You see, the mayor of Coventry wasn't a witch. He thought the festival my coven was hosting was some sort of hippie music and love fest. He had no idea the town was full of real witches. Well, half full... and that the people traveling from around the world to our new Beltane Festival were also real witches.

And so, he'd planned the ceremony to open the new sheriff's station on the same day the festival was to kick off. Thorn had tried to talk him out of it, but it wasn't like he could tell him there was a massive magical jamboree going on.

Even if he had told him, the mayor wouldn't have heard it. Or he wouldn't have processed it. You see, the thing that protected the other ordinary half of Coventry from knowing about us witches was a magic veil that covered the town. It drew power from a ley line that ran right through the center of town. And so did we. But the important part is that veil kept the normies from seeing or hearing anything they shouldn't. And it worked most of the time. People like Thorn could see partway through it. He knew something was different about Coventry even before we fell in love and I revealed the truth to him. Fortunately, he accepted that the world wasn't as it appeared, and after some time and trials, he eventually wholly accepted who I was too.

But that veil wasn't the same as the veil that separated the living from the dead. That's a whole other veil. It's complicated... But not that complicated. Two veils. One that keeps the townsfolk of Coventry from seeing us do witchy sh... stuff... and ghosts... and anything else paranormal. The other one separates the living world from the other side.

And I was beginning to worry that Hekate, who loved to mess around with the veil between the living and dead, had shoved my book through to the other side in retaliation for me making her clean her room. She was six, but you'd swear she was sixteen sometimes.

"Third grade sucks," I heard Laney telling Hekate in between rinse and spits. "I can't wait until I'm in fourth grade. Then we'll be the real big kids."

"At least you're not a first grader," Hekate lamented. "The only kids at the school who are bigger babies are the kindergarteners."

"Can you make sure they don't have toothpaste on their shirts before you leave?" I asked Thorn who was making his way over to me.

"I can help you look," he relented. "This is more important that a stupid grand opening for our station."

"No, it's not," I said, but it totally was… "Just check and make sure they haven't made a mess of themselves, and then I'll see you later?"

"Sure thing, Boss Lady," he said and pulled me into his arms.

I should have protested the long, deep kiss he bestowed on me, but it was actually the pause I needed to pull myself together. He was good like that.

Once we parted, Thorn checked the girls and then made his way downstairs. I kept looking for the book that had the ritual I needed to open the festival. A witch from England had sent it to me as a gift. It was an ancient grimoire with all sorts of old-world rituals. And of course, I could find the box she'd shipped it in, but I could not find the book.

I was about to call out to the girls and ask them if they'd done something mischievous, when Thorn called upstairs to me. "Kinsley, someone's at the door for you!"

"Oh, man. Honey, I don't have time!" I said and knelt down to look under the bed. Hey, you never knew...

But as I was pushing back the black bedspread, Thorn called up again. "I think you're going to want to make time. It's your mother."

"Mom!" I said and jumped up. "Oh, gawd, yes! Girls, Grandma is here!"

Suddenly, all of their grumbling turned to happiness and giggles. They quickly finished up in the bathroom and nearly ran me over trying to get downstairs to Grandma.

"Mom," I said as I descended the stairs after them. "Mom, you are a goddess among women."

"Wow, that's quite the greeting," she said.

"She can't find the book," Thorn said as he put on his hat. "Good morning, Brighton. You truly are a sight for sore eyes."

"Flattery will get you everywhere," Mom said as Thorn kissed her on the cheek.

They had been good friends before I came back to town. Thorn was actually Thorn Jr., and he was the son of the man my mother had nearly ended up with. Except that Thorn Sr. was a sociopath who broke her heart. Well, he tried to break her heart. Turned out that it had always belonged to my father, Remy, anyway. And as soon as Thorn Sr. left Coventry, my father and mother had begun their happy ever after.

But when Thorn Jr. had turned up in town one day as the new sheriff, my parents had embraced him with open arms. I hadn't taken to him quite as easily. But after my own sociopathic vampire sort-of-husband tried to

7

break my heart, Thorn and I started our happy ever after.

"Have a good day," I said as he kissed me again and then headed out.

Per the usual ritual, the girls ran out the door after him. The followed him to his cruiser and made sure they were the last to give him kisses before he left for work.

"I'll take them to school," Mom said, "so you can finish getting ready. It's a big day."

"Thank you so much," I said and hugged her. "I'm sorry I didn't just ask for your help, but I thought I could do it all on my own."

Mom smiled. "The other day you mentioned taking the book into the shop so that you could pick up the last of what you needed."

I snapped my fingers. "That's right. I can't believe I would just leave it there."

"Go finish getting ready. I'll get the girls off to school, and then you can run by the shop on your way to the festival grounds."

"What if it's not there?" I asked.

"I'm sure it is," Mom answered. "But if it's not, we'll just do a little divination to find it."

"I probably should have started with that," I lamented.

"You've got a lot on your plate," she said. "Now go! I'll get the girls breakfast, and you go take your ritual shower."

"Thank you so much," I said.

With that, I kissed her on the cheek and darted up the stairs.

"Girls, come inside for breakfast!" I heard Mom shout out the door to the girls as I closed the bedroom door.

Before I could get it closed all of the way, a large, dark shadow bolted in. It jumped up into the middle of the bed and stared at me with huge yellow eyes.

"You're an idiot," Meri groused.

"Not as dumb as you," I said and went to my closet to grab a bottle of cleansing ritual shower gel.

"I'm not the one who lost the book I need to open a huge ceremony. Witches have come from all over the world, and you just oopsied and lost an ancient grimoire."

"Shouldn't you take some of the blame for this?" I asked as I emerged from the closet. "You're supposed to be my familiar. Like protect me and accentuate my magic powers. Why don't you know where the book is?"

"Did you check in the attic library?" he asked without answering my question.

"I never took it up there," I said. "Mom thinks I left it at the shop, but I'll check up there before I leave."

"I'll go," he groused. "I'll check the attic while you get ready."

"Why are you being so helpful now?" I asked skeptically.

"Just open the door," he snarked, and I did.

As soon as I did, the smell of cooking bacon wafted in from downstairs. "Oh, that's why," I chuckled. "You realized you got yourself trapped in here when there's bacon downstairs."

"Whatever," he retorted. "I said I'd check, and I'll check."

"Whatever," I responded and closed the door. As snarky and ill-tempered as he could be, I could trust him to check the attic for me.

I wanted to shower quickly and get moving with my day, but I knew that morning, my morning ritual was just as important as any other I'd perform. If I was quick or sloppy, my haste could negatively affect the festival. So I forced myself to slow down as much as I could.

By the time I was out and getting dressed, the house was nearly silent. My mother and the girls must have already gone off to school.

So I pulled my favorite black tank top and ankle-length skirt from the closet. It was a simple outfit, but I dressed it up with a crescent moon pendant and earrings. The pendant hung down to the middle of my chest, so I had room to layer more necklaces. I added a couple of delicate silver box chains and a smaller pendant that represented the three phases of the moon. The middle moon was a gleaming white opal.

After pulling my curly red hair up into a messy bun, I'd need it out of my face to keep from going insane, I spritzed it with gardenia hair perfume. A touch of jet-black mascara and a swipe of blood-red lip tint was all I needed to complete the look.

"You look hideous," Meri said when I opened the bedroom door.

He sat there staring up at me. "So do you," I said and stepped over him.

That part had become a great deal more difficult. During Meri's tenure as my familiar, he'd magically been turned into a tiny kitten twice. He'd hated it, but I'd thought it was hilarious. Since the last mishap, though, he'd been transformed into a giant black Maine coon. Meri was even bigger and more majestic than when he'd become my familiar. And of course, it had gone straight to his head.

"I need bacon," he said, and I stopped at the top of the stairs.

"You had breakfast. I know my mom fed you," I said before resuming my way downstairs.

"No, she didn't," he lied.

"Whatever," I said. "Come on, then."

"She did feed me," he confessed as he trailed down the stairs behind me. One of the benefits of him being in servitude to my family was that he couldn't really lie to me. Not that I cared anyway. I would give him more bacon.

"I know," I responded. "But today is a big day. Let's make sure you are good and fortified for everything we have in store."

"Now that sounds like a plan."

We went into the kitchen, and Mom had washed her breakfast dishes. I took two frying pans out of the dish rack and started heating them up on the stove. I'd mostly use magic to cook the food because we were in a hurry, but a little mundane support didn't hurt anything.

I quickly fried up some bacon for myself and made pancakes with instant mix and a handful of chocolate chips. I made a few extra pancakes and put them in the fridge for Bonkers. Our household had another familiar. His name was Bonkers, and he was a fat orange cat with a lazy eye. He could also consume demons and bad spirits like they were candy. And he loved carbs. Bonkers thought Meri's bacon addiction was gross.

But Bonkers mostly stuck to Laney's side. He was her familiar, and as such, went to school with her every day. He and Meri were decently good friends, but as Laney grew older, Bonkers stayed glued to her.

It was just a good thing that the magical school in Coventry had been expanded from a preschool to a school for witches of all ages. That meant familiars could attend classes with their masters and mistresses. Hekate as of yet had not found a familiar, but she was all right with that. Though I had seen a crow hanging around Hangman's House recently, and I'd begun to wonder if it was watching her out of more than curiosity.

Hangman's House was my house, by the way. Because of course I lived in a house that had a name. And it was such named because Coventry had a dark past. Before the witches took over the town, they'd been hunted. We'd had our own version of the Salem Witch Trials, and the man who hung our ancestor sisters had lived in my home.

But we'd reclaimed it. First was my mother when she returned to Coventry decades before. Then she passed the house to me when I returned home and became leader of our coven. And just for good measure, there was a cemetery hidden in the woods across the street. The oldest part held the remains of some of the most powerful witches from our families, and when needed, they would rise up and protect me and my family.

As I hurried out to my car to head to my shop, Summoned Goods & Sundries, I asked for their blessing. A warm wind caressed my face and carried the scent of rosemary and peppermint.

"Thank you," I responded before getting into the car and heading off for my day.

Chapter Two

Summoned Goods & Sundries wasn't my only business. Across the square was Craft Donuts, and it had a line out the door. Fortunately, we'd prepared for the festival crowd, and my staff was all hands on deck. I knew it was frantic, but they could handle it. Next door to Craft Donuts was my friend Viv's coffee house, Brew Station. They also had a line out the door, but I knew she was loving it.

What I wouldn't have given for a hazelnut latte, but I wasn't sure I had time to stand in line. I told myself that if the book was at the shop, I'd stop over at the Brew Station and check out the line. A caffeinated witch was an effective witch, and I owed it to all of the Coventry witches, and those who had traveled to our fair town, to be at my best. I wasn't sure I could do that without one of Viv's hazelnut lattes. I looked at my watch. If the line moved quickly, I still had time.

There was no line out the door of Summoned Goods & Sundries, but the place was bustling. Thankfully, over the last few years, we'd expanded. I'd taken the money I made from the shop and bought the building. Not renting anymore allowed me to also purchase the building next door and knock out the wall between them. The large space downstairs was where all the tourists shopped. I'd turned the upstairs apartments into the "witch only" area of the store. Previously, it had been in the back of the shop, and the veil kept tourists from wandering back there. That and some strong warding to reinforce the veil's powers. Coventry's ley line ran right through the square, and since my shops were on the square, I could draw an awesome amount of power from it.

But back to the tourists. Coventry's tourism industry had only grown over the years. People visited us for historical tours and haunted history walks. The witch trials, along with plenty of internet rumors about ghosts and witches, drew people in from all over the world. Of course, they never found anything concrete, but the rumors never stopped. Nor did the tourism dollars. Coventry had grown so much over the last few years that it had begun to stretch the definition of a small town, but we had maintained that small-town look and feel.

And the rumor mill. We'd never outgrow that.

Inside the shop, all three of my employees were hard at work. Sol Mallor was behind the front counter ringing out customer purchases. Azura Le Blank was on the floor helping a couple of women, whose attire and wide-eyed wonder screamed tourist, pick out a spell bag to go along with their crystal purchases. I didn't see Estrella Delarosa-Skeenbauer, but I figured she was upstairs helping witches select last-minute supplies for the festival.

I also didn't see Reggie, my best friend, store manager, and business partner, but I had no idea where she would be. The most likely place would've been the back office, but I couldn't see her hanging back there while the store was so busy. She took running Summoned very seriously.

Still, I figured it would be the logical first place to check, so I hurried through the small crowd of tourists, dodged the checkout line, and headed to the back. But not before stopping for a second to say good morning to Sol and Azura.

"Good morning, guys. You two doing okay?" I asked.

"Having a wonderful day," Sol said with a cheerful wave.

He lived up to his name. Sol was a light witch who had embraced his powers like a champion. He also dressed the part. While Azura had chosen a black long-sleeved shirt and black slacks for work that day, Sol had donned a lemon-yellow polo shirt and pressed khakis. The only thing that made him look remotely like he belonged working in the shop was the septum piercing in his nose and the sun tattooed on the side of his neck. But his sweet nature and charming demeanor made those physical distinctions almost cute.

Azura was nearly the polar opposite. She was polite and good with the customers, but she had an edge. Her nose piercing and neck tattoo of a crow made her look slightly menacing. Not enough that customers steered clear of her, but it was just enough that nobody gave her any guff. The cutest thing was that the two of them were a thing. They didn't think anybody knew, but we all knew. But they wanted it to be a secret, so we all pretended we didn't know.

"It has been a good morning," Azura added. She glanced over at Sol furtively before continuing, "are you ready for the big festival, boss?"

"I am, and I hope you guys are planning on coming once the shop closes," I said.

"We wouldn't miss it for the world," Sol answered.

I'd considered closing the shop for the festival, but I ran a witch shop... during a witch festival... it would have been madness to close. Not only was I the premier location in Coventry for magical goods and sundries, but the Beltane Festival had attracted a ton of tourists too. I would have been throwing away a fortune, and the witches of Coventry would have had nowhere to do their last-minute preparations.

After another minute or so of polite chitchat, I excused myself past the line and through the store. As soon as I stepped into the back storage room, Reggie appeared from the staff bathroom. She wore a floor-length black ballgown embroidered with silver moons and stars. She'd swept her golden hair up into a fancy French twist with just a few tendrils loose to frame her face.

"You look beautiful," I said, "but you cannot be serious."

"It is gorgeous, isn't it?" She beamed proudly. "I had it custom made. Jeremy nearly threw a fit until I reminded him that I have given him three sons in the last three years."

It was true, the two of them had had three sons nearly one right after another, and those boys were everything to her husband Jeremy, who also happened to be Thorn's undersheriff. Reggie and Jeremy were like family to me, and I considered Maddock, Leif, and Tierney to be my nephews.

"It's gorgeous, and you're even more beautiful," I gushed. Because she was. Even after three kids, Reggie had abs and a butt you could bounce a quarter off of, and while part of that was a magic spell my family had bestowed on her years before, she was also just naturally beautiful. "But that dress cannot be what I think it is."

"I told you I was entering the Flower Queen Pageant," she huffed. "I told you like a million times."

"Yeah, but Reggie, I thought you were joking. The pageant is part of the festival. It's for witches."

She pouted. "Are you going to bar me from entering?"

"No," I said with a chuckle because I could never do that to her. "But, Reggie, a witch is going to win. They're going to know you're not, and I just don't want you to be disappointed."

"I don't care," she said defiantly. "I want to do the pageant. If you're not going to stop me, nothing will."

Far be it from me to tell a woman in her forties, wearing a floor-length ballgown she had custom made, that she couldn't enter a pageant. Fortunately, because of the spell my family had endowed upon her, Reggie didn't look like she was in her forties. She would blend in perfectly with all of the younger witches who'd entered. Our friend Viv had also received the blessing, so the three of us appeared to be in our early twenties at most.

"Well, even if you can't win, you're going to knock them dead," I said, and she beamed again.

"Really?"

"Yeah, I mean, I've had a chance to see some of the competition and their dresses, and you're going to put a lot of younger women to shame, my dear."

"I should take this off so nothing happens to it," she said and turned to head back into the bathroom.

I whispered a protection spell under my breath to preserve the dress for her, but said, "That's a good idea."

"I'll be right back."

"Wait, one second," I said because I did need to get going. Especially if there was going to be a latte in my future.

"Yes?" Reggie asked from the bathroom doorway.

"I need to find my book. The grimoire from England. I need it to open the festival. Have you seen it?"

"Top desk drawer," Reggie said. "I found it upstairs next to the belladonna berries. You must have left it."

"Oh, thank you!" I said.

"Don't you dare leave without me," Reggie said before closing the bathroom door.

I guessed that meant we were going to the festival together. I couldn't tell her she had to stay and work. Fortunately for Reggie, the same sigil she wore that allowed her to pass into the "witches only" part of the store would also get her through the barrier around the festival. Around the outside edges of the festival were areas where non-witches could gather and even partake in some festivities, but to get into the real stuff, you had to be a witch. Or have a sigil that allowed you to pass because you were best friends with the witch in charge.

"Fine, I'll wait," I called out loud enough for her to hear me in the bathroom. "But get a move on. I want to try to get a latte before we head over to the grounds."

"Oh, are you buying?" Reggie hollered back.

"Always," I replied and hoped it got her to hurry.

While she was in the bathroom, I went into my office and found the book in my desk drawer. I wrapped it in a black ceremonial cloth, and then slipped it into my messenger bag of supplies. Since Reggie was still changing, I ran upstairs really quick and grabbed some more of the belladonna berries. We'd need them for ceremonial tea, and I was nervous I didn't have enough.

Once I was back downstairs, I found Reggie zipping her gown into its garment bag. "Let's rock and roll," I said. "I don't think we have time for coffee, but I want to try anyway."

I waved goodbye to everyone on my way out. Estrella had made her way downstairs by the time we were leaving, and I saw that she was having a conversation with Madeline Skeenbauer, her mother-in-law. Madeline must have dropped in to grab last-minute supplies and boy, did she need a lot. She and Estrella had filled two large shopping bags with herbs and more. Madeline wouldn't wait in line with the tourists to check out, though. Estrella would take her payment for the goods. Witches could pay with money or the promise of favors. I took either, but only from witches. Regular folks paid with cash or credit cards.

"Don't you want to put that somewhere?" I asked Reggie as we hurried across the square. She was struggling to carry the dress and keep up with me. If she didn't have anywhere to put it, I was going to take it from her. A little magic and the thing would practically float behind me. There was no point in making her work so hard.

"I forgot to put it in your car," she said. "Mine's on the other side of the square, though. I'll chuck it in until we've got our coffee."

"Are you actually planning on riding with me?" I asked. "Don't you want to have your car in case you need to leave?"

"Ugh, you ruin everything with logic," she said. "Fine, I'll put it in my car, and I'll drive myself to the festival grounds."

"I mean, you can ride with me if you want, but I can't leave."

"No, you're right. I'll just follow you."

"At least we get to take advantage of the VIP parking," I said as we hurried past the founder's statue in the middle of the square.

Unlike most towns, Coventry's founders were women. Witches, to be exact. The ancestors who would eventually split into the Tuttlesmith and Skeenbauer witches. The two families had feuded for many decades, but my mother brought them all back together. And I was the capstone in the united coven. Tuttlesmith witches had all abandoned the craft in years past, but my mom and I had brought the lineage back. My daughters would carry Tuttlesmith blood into the ages.

"I'm going to take advantage of everything VIP while I'm with you," Reggie quipped.

"As you should," I agreed.

From wherever he'd run off to when I'd gone into the shop, Meri returned. He darted across the town square from the north, and the direction of our courthouse, to join Reggie and me.

The line was shorter than when I'd gone into Summoned Goods & Sundries, but it was still out the door. I wasn't sure we'd have time to wait, but I figured I'd give it a couple of minutes. Maybe the line was moving fast...

But as soon as I got behind the last woman in line, she stepped out of the way. And then everyone in front of her did too.

It was then I realized they were all witches. Well, a couple of them might have been confused tourists, but they just did what everyone else did.

"You guys don't have to do this," I said.

"Look at the time, Kinsley," one of them said. "We don't want you to have to go without your coffee, but you have to go."

And she was right. I still didn't want to cut in front of everyone, but Reggie made that a little easier. She pushed past me, grabbed my hand, and dragged me up to the front counter.

On the way, we passed one of my other best friends, Dorian. Dressed in a gray Henley, jeans, and black work boots, he was seated at a table pecking away at his laptop, but as soon as he saw us, he snapped it closed and shot out of his chair. He swept a lock of hair from his face and tucked it behind his ear. His hair wasn't quite to his shoulders yet, but he'd let it grow out lately. I laughed as he said, "I'm with you guys," and joined us at the counter.

"My favorite people in the world!" Viv announced when she turned around and saw us at the counter. "Oh, but Kinsley, I didn't expect to see you today. You've got to hurry."

"I know," I responded sheepishly.

Viv clapped her hands. "Anna, get Dorian a refill to go. Finn, prepare a peaches and cream white chocolate mocha for Reggie, and Beck, make Kinsley her hazelnut latte with a double pump and extra cream."

"You're the best," I said. "Really, just the best."

"I'll see you tonight?" Viv asked. "Or late this afternoon if I can slip out early. Once the day rush dies down, I think Beck can take over."

"Oh, right," I said and fished a bracelet out of my purse. It had the same sigil on it that Reggie used to get into witch spaces. It would allow Vivian to get in anywhere at the festival when she met us later.

"I'm sorry I have to run out," I said when Viv's employees handed over our drinks.

"Nonsense, you're the queen today, and I'll see you later."

"Thank you so much," I said and left a couple of twenties in the tip jar.

"I'm riding with you," Dorian said as we left the Brew Station.

"I'll tell you the same thing I told Reggie. I'd love to have you, but I can't leave. If you ride with me, you're stuck unless you find another way home."

"Where am I going to go anyway? I have to be there to do a write-up. It's in my blood," Dorian said.

"Remember what I told you, and I mean it."

"I know, I know. I can only put what I write in a fiction story. No news or blog articles," Dorian relented.

Dorian was a reporter and fiction author. He'd moved to Coventry and restarted the old newspaper as well as establishing an internet presence for it. He loved to be right in the middle of anything he considered a "story," and I loved him for that, but he absolutely could not publish anything about the festival as nonfiction.

Just then, Viv came running out of the shop. She shoved two bags of bacon into my hand. "You forgot," she said with a wink.

I looked down and saw Meri scowl at me. But he was relieved that Viv had remembered and rewarded her with a rub against her legs.

"Thank you," I said.

"Knock 'em dead, Queen," she said and kissed me on the cheek before rushing back inside.

"Follow me," I said to Reggie and blew her a kiss.

"You ready for this?" Dorian asked.

Before I could answer, a dark cloud rolled overhead, and thunder crashed through the square.

Awesome.

Chapter Three

"Nice weather we're having," Dorian joked through a strained smile.

Lightning flashed again and a crack of thunder rolled across the sky.

"No... no... no..." I muttered as I tried to focus on my driving. "What did I do?"

"What do you mean, what did you do?" Dorian asked.

"This idiot messed up her morning," Meri piped up from the back seat. "And now the festival is about to get rained out."

"How do you mess up your morning?" Dorian asked with genuine concern, but I could also tell he was mentally taking notes. "You're alive. You're on your way. What was there to mess up?"

"It's hard to explain," I said.

"Well, try. I've been your friend for years, Kinsley. I know the ins and outs of your witchy business at this point, and don't forget that I have my own experience with the occult."

Ah, yes, Dorian's experience with the occult... Dorian's a former werewolf. How could he be former? Well, because he wasn't born a shifter. Dorian hadn't always been a reporter for, and proprietor of, the Coventry town newspaper. When he was younger, he was an investigative journalist. One of his investigations took him deep into the Satanic Church. Somehow, he'd allowed himself to get sucked in entirely and went all the way to the top level. At that point, you had to choose the path of blood or path of flesh. That meant becoming a vampire or werewolf through demonic means. Dorian chose werewolf and got himself a spiffy demon wolf that melded with his soul.

Because he knew the occult, when he realized what he'd done and wanted to find a way out, he was able to get a witch to help him trap that wolf in a mirror. In the end, I helped him destroy the demon wolf and freed him.

We'd been bestest friends ever since. The whole Satanic Church-werewolf-demon thing had put a strain on his marriage to his husband, Isaac, but they had reconciled. And then they ended up divorced anyway. That was a long story in itself, but he was doing fine. Isaac had never truly forgiven him, and it had left a dark cloud of stress over their home. But those clouds had lifted when Isaac left Coventry, and Dorian was like a new man. Again...

"Please don't remind me of that," I said with a nervous chuckle. "We don't need to bring any of that evil into this day."

"If I didn't know you any better, I'd say that you were saying I'm bad luck," Dorian said with a huff, but the twinkle in his eye told me he was joking.

We turned down the country road that led to the festival grounds, and sprinkles of light rain pattered on the windshield. I cracked the window, and the smell of ozone and petrichor filled the car. If it was going to rain, I was going to enjoy it.

"I don't think this will be so bad," Dorian said after a few minutes. "I mean, you guys are witches. You love all of this nature stuff, right? That includes the rain?"

"As long as it doesn't storm so badly we have to cancel," I sighed.

"If it rains, I'm staying in the car," Meri announced.

"You're my familiar, and this is one of the biggest events of my life... I mean, as far as witch stuff goes... you're going to be by my side."

"You're nuts, lady," Meri groused. "I didn't come here to follow your boring behind around for days."

"Meri," I warned.

"Whatever. What are you going to do about it?"

"I'll get Lilith to put you in a jar," I answered matter-of-factly as we drove onto the festival grounds.

"I could get out," he responded.

"Could you, though?" I drove through the parking area, which was already filling up, to the area set aside for VIPs.

"Fine," he relented. "I guess I can make an appearance."

"The clouds seem to be letting up too," Dorian said as I parked the car next to Reggie's. She'd beaten us there by moments.

"Just a little extra excitement to start the day," I said warily. "Can you keep an eye on the weather forecasts for me, though?" I asked Dorian.

"Oh, I have an official job now?"

"Dude, if you thought I wasn't going to put you to work, you don't know me very well. You want to hang around and get all the juicy details of this festival, then you're my personal assistant."

"Well, then… Okay, boss. I'll keep an eye on the weather and any other tasks you might have for me."

"Good," I said with a chuckle. "All right, let's do this."

I felt a little lift to my spirits when I stepped out of the car, and the clouds parted. The sun shone down and warmed my face while a gentle breeze caught my hair and clothes. I stopped, closed my eyes, and took it all in. The sounds of laughter filled the air instead of thunder. The festival hadn't even started yet, but there was joy everywhere. Oh, and the smell of food too.

Not only were there dozens of vendors set up selling everything from breakfast sandwiches to those mini state fair donuts, but there were people who had brought grills and were tailgating. The scents of burgers, bacon, coffee, and cinnamon sugar were heavy in the air. I felt my stomach rumble in anticipation even thought I'd just eaten. I could always eat again. Always.

It was about that time that we stepped out from behind a tent and I saw how many witches were gathered for the festival. It made my stomach clench, and I even felt a little woozy.

Dorian reached out and grabbed my shoulder. "Are you okay?" he asked. "You got really pale."

"So many people," I said... well, mostly mumbled.

Dorian looked out at the crowd. "Oh, come on, Kinsley. You can handle this. You're basically the queen of these people."

"That's what terrifies me," I squeaked out. "My coven I can handle. I'm used to that. I've never seen this many witches in one place, though."

"You basically rule Coventry too," Dorian added. "There are way more people in Coventry than are at this festival."

I took a deep breath and looked at him with wide eyes. I had no idea why I was freaking out, but there we were. And it was happening.

"Okay," Dorian said and looked at his watch. "We have maybe fifteen to twenty minutes before you have to be on that stage. What would make you feel better?"

"A snack," I said without missing a beat.

Dorian sighed and rolled his eyes, but he eventually smiled. "At least you're easy."

"Hey," I said and punched him playfully in the arm.

"What? It's true. I'm not insulting you, but it's not like you asked me to go out into this crowd and find you some sort of confidence potion."

"There's probably a vendor selling them," I said as I started toward the row of food stalls.

"Isn't that like... drugs?" Dorian asked skeptically.

"I guess it is, but drugs don't affect us the way they do humans. We have a lot more control over the way they affect us. You know that. Besides, it's a festival."

"So you do want drugs?" Dorian cocked an eyebrow.

"No, I want one of those honey cornbread rolls," I said and pointed toward a stall. "I bet they are just as good as drugs."

"Let's go," he said and took me by the hand.

Dorian led me through the crowd so fast that I practically had to run to keep up. Though I would have been loath to admit it, the whole thing was kind of exhilarating. My heartrate picked up as our pace quickened, and I quickly forgot about my anxiety.

Don't get me wrong, when we got to the stall, I still got the muffin. Dorian got one too. He laughed as I shoved half of it in my mouth.

After a cup of hot cider, I felt ready to go. "I can do this," I said to Dorian as he took the last bite of his muffin.

"You sure you don't want to get a bacon, egg, and cheese sandwich or something?" he asked with a laugh. "Maybe a hot fudge sundae? Someone brought an ice cream truck... but is that pot leaf next to the menu?"

"Don't tempt me because I totally do, but I think I can wait," I said ignoring his question about the ice cream truck because it was a pot leaf. Apparently, you could get your ice cream with or without edibles.

"I can't," Meri said. "Get me some bacon."

"We have five minutes," Dorian said.

"It's fine. I'll go up to the stage and get ready to open the festival. You get Meri his bacon and meet me up there."

"Are you sure?" Dorian asked.

"I need him at his best, and I feel bad for eating without getting him something."

"You spoil that cat."

"Hey, I'm right here, dog boy," Meri groused. "I'll be fine without the bacon. This is important."

I smiled down at him. "You sure?"

"Don't ask me that again. You'll be going on that stage alone."

"You are such a butt," I said.

"Whatever," Meri countered.

I didn't want to stand there arguing with him about bacon when the festival opening ceremony was to begin in minutes. I'd already spent too much time emotional eating honey cornbread rolls.

"Let's do this," I said with slightly more confidence than I felt.

I made my way to the main stage, which was basically just a huge wooden platform about waist high off the ground, and climbed up the stairs. When I looked out over the grounds, I began to get a little woozy again. But Dorian walked around to the front and stood right in the center. I felt Meri rub against my leg, and that was all I needed. Well, it would have been nice if Reggie was around, but she'd probably taken her dress to the pageant area so it wouldn't get wrinkled from being stuffed in her car. Plus, she wasn't a witch, so her being present for the opening of the festival wasn't entirely necessary.

When the other witches saw me on the stage and Dorian standing at the front, they quickly figured out that it was time to gather round. I was happy to see that they calmly made their way to the front, for the most part. It was obvious that some of them had already had a little too much confidence potion, but the rowdy ones stayed around the edges. Thankfully, they kept their whooping and tambourine playing to a minimum as I stepped forward to speak.

My voice wavered just as Reggie came hurrying across a patch of grass to my right. I smiled when she took her place next to Dorian.

"I want to welcome everyone to Coventry's First Annual Beltane Festival," I called out to the rapt audience. "We're about to light the first fires, and I'd like for everyone to focus their intentions on us having a safe, sane, but amazingly good time."

Everyone turned to the giant stacks of woods nearest to them. We had seven total all placed a few hundred feet away from the stage.

I took the ancient grimoire out of my bag and unwrapped it. I had the page I needed marked with a red ribbon. I opened it and swallowed my nerves. I could do this. I was born to do this.

I was just about to start reading the ritual I'd chosen as the opening ceremony when a scream rang out like a gong.

A hush fell over the entire crowd. Even the tambourine players stopped and started looking around for the source of the shriek.

"Is everyone all right?" I said once I got my racing heart under control. "Does somebody need help?"

"He's dead!" a woman's voice called out from the same general direction of the scream.

"Oh, here we go," Meri groused.

"Not helping," I said as I left the stage and hurried toward the spot where the crowd had both parted and was gathering. "What is going on?" I called out to the people standing in the inside of the circle.

"He's really dead," one of the witches said. "What is this?"

The woman turned a little green and stumbled backwards. It was then I realized she was heavily intoxicated. Completely inebriated and in shock, so she'd probably forgotten that she could pull herself together with nothing more than her intentions. I had to remember that not all of the witches around me were as accomplished and serious about the craft as the witches of Coventry.

"Someone get her some water," I said as her friends practically carried her through the crowd.

I quickly rewrapped the grimoire and tucked it into my bag. The last thing I wanted was to lose or damage such a precious gift in the kerfuffle.

"Yep, that's a body," Meri said as I breached the scene.

"What the fu... heck!" slipped out. It wasn't just a body. It was a whole... scene. A man stabbed with a knife surrounded by a circle of black salt. I turned away to catch my breath. I couldn't believe it was happening again.

Suddenly, Dorian and Reggie were on either side of me. Reggie wound her arm around mine. Dorian went to step in front of me, but my other arm shot out to keep him from getting too close. He was so protective, even if it was just to shield me from something causing me distress.

"I'm okay," I said reading his intentions. "Don't get too close. We don't want to mess up the evidence."

"How did this happen right here?" he asked.

"Who did this?" I asked the crowd, but I knew the question was in vain. "Did anybody see anything?"

"How did they do this right here?" Dorian seemed shaken.

"Look," I said and pointed toward tent stakes. "They were in a tent that I assume they ripped down when they left. Plus, we're sort of back between two food stands. It is totally possible no one saw anything," I admitted.

"We walked right by here minute ago," Dorian said.

"Keep it together," I said.

"I'm fine," he said. "It's just... this isn't normal witchcraft. It's not, right?"

"We should do something to cover him up," Reggie said. "People are going to freak out."

"We can't disturb the scene," I answered.

"Come on, Kinsley. This guy is surrounded by witches. You can't possibly think that there's going to be any kind of useable forensic evidence anyway."

She had a point. I looked around to see if anyone was... I didn't even know. Smiling? Looking proud? All I saw was either repulsion from those close or curiosity from anyone who wasn't close enough to see what had happened to the man.

"Your husband is going to shut the festival down," Dorian said.

"I can talk him out of it. We just need to shut down this area until they are done, and then everything can proceed. We don't need to cancel the entire festival."

The two women running the food stalls nearby looked stricken. It was obvious that the murder, and there was no doubt in my mind it was a murder, was going to severely affect their business until we got the scene cleared.

"There are three or four bar stalls on the other side of the food area that won't be in use until tonight. Can I get some volunteers to help these women move their operations over there?" I asked.

"I can wrangle that," Reggie stepped forward.

"Good," I said with a nod. Reggie was nothing if not a good manager. She wasn't a witch, but I had no doubt she could have the women back up and running in no time. "Okay," I announced as loudly as I could, "I need everyone to push back from the scene. I need as many of you as possible to meet Reggie behind these food stalls and help her move products to the new location. Pretty soon, we're going to have the sheriff and his deputies here, and I need everyone to cooperate and give them space to work. Since my husband is the sheriff, I think I can convince him to let us keep the festival open, but I need everyone here right now to work together."

Chapter Four

"Absolutely not," Thorn said with his fists planted firmly on his hips. "I get why you're asking, but you know I can't do that."

"Thorn..." I started to restate my case, but he cut me off.

"Kinsley, no. This is... Well, I don't know what this is, but it's serious. I might have to call in the FBI."

"No!" I exclaimed and grabbed his bicep so hard Thorn winced. "You cannot call in the FBI. This is... it is something else, but you can handle it. We can handle it."

"You have to admit that this looks like the work of some sick, twisted serial killer," Jeremy, Thorn's undersheriff, interjected. "It looks to me like someone took advantage of the crowd, although I still don't know how, and carried out some sort of sick ritual."

"Ha!" I said and wondered if the stress was unhinging me a little. "Even you admit that this looks like a ritual. Hence, it's my jurisdiction."

Thorn almost laughed, but when he remembered that I could put him in a jar and keep him as a pretty little decoration on our mantle, he stifled it, then narrowed his piercing blue eyes to let me know he was super serious. "Kinsley, you don't have a jurisdiction."

"Hey, now. We witches deserve magical representation. Just because up until now, we haven't had it, that doesn't mean we shouldn't."

Thorn pinched the bridge of his nose the way he did a lot more since I'd embraced my magical place in the world. You see, at one time, I'd run away from Coventry. And even when I returned, I was determined to make magic as little a part of my life, and the lives of all of Coventry's witches, as I could. But in recent years, spending more time with my mother and my Auntie Lilith had led to a magical awakening in my soul.

And sometimes, I annoyed my husband with it.

"Kinsley, I admire your... honey, I don't know... but I admire it. Unfortunately, this isn't the time or place."

"Her spirit," Jeremy interjected. "She's a spunky thing," he said with a wink.

"Thanks," I said and gave Jeremy a high five, but Thorn was right.

"Please don't encourage her," Thorn said with a deep, shuddering sigh. "You work for me, remember."

"Okay, fine," I relented because I could see I was more than stressing Thorn out, and I didn't want to start a rift between him and Jeremy. Especially when Jeremy wasn't really encouraging me. He was just trying to lighten the mood. As was his way. "But this festival is a big deal for me," I continued. "It's a big deal for all of us. Especially the witches who traveled all over the world to be here. My coven will never live down the international humiliation of being shut down by MY husband."

Thorn took another deep breath and opened his mouth to speak. Then he snapped it shut and took another long inhalation through his nose. Whatever he was originally going to say, he thought better of it.

"You don't have to say it like that," Thorn said softly. "Like this is my fault? You cannot put this on me."

I felt a stab of guilt. "I'm sorry, Thorn. I didn't mean it like *that*. But you have to try to see it from my perspective too. I know things are a little more traditionally human in our home but think of how most of these women would view me letting my husband tell me what to do. It's unheard of in some parts of the world. I'm probably losing some of their respect even having this conversation with you instead of just sending you away without an explanation."

"Wow," Jeremy said and rubbed his neck nervously. "You guys are into some strange stuff."

"It's not that strange," Thorn said in defense, and it made the butterflies in my stomach do a little dance. "Just because human men have lorded over women for all of human history... I think these witches have it right. The world would be a better place if men listened to women." He was so getting some extra lovin' for that one.

Another one of the deputies joined us just then. He didn't seem to notice Thorn calling us all witches. Thanks to the veil, he'd most likely heard something else. Like the word women instead, or he'd heard an entirely different conversation.

Realization spread across Thorn's face. If all of his deputies, minus himself and Jeremy who knew all about witches, couldn't see through the veil, how were they even supposed to investigate the murder? He needed me.

And it also made zero sense to call in the FBI. Thank the Goddess for that.

"Give me a couple of hours to get everything straight," Thorn relented. "You don't have to send everyone away, but I'm going to cordon off a wide area for my deputies and the coroner to work. And please keep things as quiet and calm as possible," he halfway pleaded with me as the sound of a tambourine rang out once from somewhere a few hundred feet away.

"You heard the man!" I called out. "And if you didn't, let me repeat it. We're going to give the sheriff and deputies their space. Please be as respectful as you can so that we don't have to shut the festival grounds down for the entire day, and then when these fine law enforcement officers are done with their work, the festival will continue as planned."

It was a good thing the murder had occurred on the part of the festival grounds where you didn't need a sigil to enter. The food vendors had wanted to make as much money as possible, and that meant the stalls and food trucks had to be accessible to the tourists too. We were all close enough to the outside edge to allow law enforcement to do their jobs as best they could and then get lost.

Right after my announcement, the witches surrounding me just sort of stood around and looked at each other. After a minute though, they began wandering off in the other direction towards the rest of the food stalls and the games areas. It was just in time for two of Thorn's deputies to come back from their cars with large rolls of crime scene tape.

"How festive," I groused.

"Good one," Meri added with a chuckle.

"That cat's not going to... disturb the body, is it?" One of the newer deputies asked as his face turned a pale shade of green. He'd probably only heard what he interpreted as Meri meowing.

"Hold me back," Meri said and then hissed.

"Meri, stop," I said and scooped him up into my arms. "Behave, little dude."

He hissed again. If there was one thing Meri hated, it was me calling him "little dude." There'd been more than one time in our lives that he'd been transformed into a tiny kitten either by an errant wish or disruptions in the magic around Coventry. Since those times, though, he'd been transformed into a massive Maine coon with long, shiny black hair and large soulful eyes. Those eyes helped him trick a lot of folks into parting with a piece of bacon or another delicious treat.

"I assure you that all of the animals here are well trained and will behave," I said and stroked Meri's head.

Right on cue, every familiar who'd accompanied their witch to the festival either poked their head out from behind their witch's legs or peeked around the corner from where they were gathered having their own fun. It made me chuckle, and for a second, the deputy looked stricken. I could only imagine what it was like to have hundreds of animals all turn and look at you at the same time when you weren't a witch.

But a placid calmness settled over his face as the veil scrambled the weirdness in his mind, and he turned away to return to his duties. As he wandered off, he mumbled something under his breath that I couldn't quite make out, but the gist of it was that I was awfully strange for a sheriff's wife.

I was glad Thorn had drifted off to consult with Jeremy because he would have been upset by his subordinate's comment. I took it as a compliment.

"Put me down," Meri complained.

"What? You don't like snuggles?" I asked and squeezed him tighter.

"Put me down right now, you crazy witch!"

"Right meow?" I teased, but I set him down gently at my feet.

Meri sat down between my shoes and flicked his tail back and forth. "What now?"

"I'm not sure," and I wasn't. "I feel like I should stay here and make sure everyone stays away from the cordoned area, but hopefully, none of us need a babysitter."

"Why don't you come help me with my pageant preparations?" Reggie asked. "I mean, the pageant is still happening, right?"

"It should be. The pageant was scheduled for the afternoon, so I figured they should be done with the whole murder thing by then. I still feel weird just leaving this scene, though."

"Oh, I'm staying," Dorian said as he quickly scribbled notes into his notebook. "I'll keep an eye on things and call you if you need to come back over here."

"Dorian, you cannot write about this for the paper," I said.

"Don't worry, boss. I wouldn't dream of it. These notes are strictly for a fiction project."

"Okay," I relented. "Reggie, let's go get you ready for that pageant."

The backstage area for the pageant was a large white tent with partitioned dressing areas inside. Off to the left when we entered was also a row of narrow tables with mirrors and lights. There were a few women already at the tables prepping their skin or hair with lotions and potions, and at the same time, I could see activity in some of the dressing rooms. A handful of witches had their assistants helping them get into their gowns or tie up elaborate corsets. It seemed early to get dressed, but I reasoned they were possibly doing a final fitting.

"Do you just pick one? Or are you assigned to a dressing room?" I asked as Reggie surveyed the competition.

"Didn't you plan this whole festival?" Reggie asked as she started for the makeshift dressing rooms.

"I mean, I did on a grand scale. I really had nothing to do with this pageant. No offense, but that's how you slipped in under the radar."

"You wouldn't have let me enter?" Reggie stuck out her bottom lip.

"It makes no difference, so I'm not going to answer that," I said with a chuckle. "But, no. I didn't plan this pageant in any way. There were some younger witches who wanted to do it, and a few local businesses put up the prize money, so I allowed it."

"You're not into this kind of thing. I get it," Reggie said as she dug a piece of paper out of her purse. "For the record, the dressing areas are assigned. This whole thing is being run very professionally. It's so we can set up our outfits in one dressing area and don't have to worry about moving things around. That would be too much chaos."

"Makes sense," I said.

"So this is mine," Reggie said when we arrived at dressing area seventeen. "I'm going to hang my dress in here, and then I've got some more things to get out of my car."

"I'll totally help. It gives me a reason to walk back by and check on things."

"It's also, like, a nice thing for you to help me carry things," Reggie said and poked my arm.

"You're right, and I'm sorry. I'm here to support you, Reggie. I can see how much this means to you, and I'm sorry that I'm being distracted."

"And judgmental," she added.

"Judgmental?"

"Yeah, because I'm not a witch and all that. You not wanting me here stings a little."

"Reggie, it's not that I don't want you here..."

But wasn't that it? She wasn't a witch, and the Beltane Festival was a huge witch... thing. Maybe I'd gone too far with my embrace of my covenly duties. I'd become a stick in the mud.

"I'm not saying you don't want me at the festival. Obviously, you invited all of your friends, but you wanted us to be observers. It bothers you that I entered the pageant."

"Well, you don't meet one of the main requirements," I said with an eyeroll. "But that's just a silly thing to get hung up on, isn't it?"

"A little bit considering that you didn't even want to have this pageant and you aren't invested in it any way," Reggie said with her own eyeroll. "Besides, look at these young gorgeous witches. It's not like I'm going to win, Kinsley. So, please, just let me have this little moment. Let me strut on that stage in my dress and tiara."

"You brought your own crown?"

"Of course I did. I'm not going to wait for anyone to give me one," Reggie said and snapped her fingers.

"I love you," I said and pulled her in for a hug. Somehow, she'd managed to make all the tension I'd carried dissipate like a wisp of smoke. Like magic. "Come on, let's go get your crown."

"And my makeup. Oh, and my hair stuff. And my shoes."

"Anything else?"

Reggie's stomach growled.

"Hungry?" I asked with one eyebrow cocked.

"I skipped breakfast. I didn't want to be bloated for the pageant. Also, I've been doing a protein and water fast for the last week."

"Do I even want to know what a protein and water fast is?" I asked skeptically.

"Basically, I've been living off chicken breast and water for a week."

I just stared at her.

"What?" she finally asked after squirming under my glare.

"What do you mean what? Reggie, you've been doing this protein and water fast for a week for a small-town festival pageant."

"Again, we agreed that you wouldn't judge me for taking this seriously," she said, but she suddenly leaned against the "wall" of her dressing area, threatening to topple the whole thing.

I caught her and let a little bit of healing magic disperse from my fingertips into her. It was like a little snake of white light leaving me and giving Reggie strength.

"Thanks for that," she said and ran a hand through her golden highlighted hair.

"We're going to get you something to eat," I said. "Before we lug all that stuff from your car."

"I can't. Not until after the pageant. My dress barely fits as it is," she protested.

"First of all, it doesn't matter if your dress fits if you pass out on stage. Second of all, this is a magic festival. You can eat anything you want, and it's not going to make you bloated. Unless you want it to… I'm sure there's somebody here selling that too."

"Oh, right," she said, and her pale cheeks bloomed with red.

"Besides, Reggie, the magic that keeps you looking young like us will also keep you from gaining weight. You know that."

"I didn't want to take any chances," she admitted.

"You doubt my family's magic?"

"Not at all, but even you have to admit it's gone haywire a time or two. I gained fifteen pounds while you were pregnant with Laney, and it wasn't like I was expecting too."

I wanted to say something, but she was right about that. My first pregnancy had disrupted the magic in Coventry, and though I didn't like to think about it, that disruption had most likely nearly gotten me killed. Thank Goddess for Meri.

"I didn't know you gained weight when that happened," I answered.

"Well, you had bigger things going on. Plus, I apparently carried it well."

"Bigger things going on than your butt?" Meri said as he sidled into the dressing tent.

"Hey!" Reggie protested.

"Kinsley is just being nice. You looked like a parade float."

I felt my eyes go as wide as saucers when I looked down to glare at Meri. He always knew the exact wrong thing to say. "Meri, stop! No, she did not!"

"Whatever," he said and turned to dart out of the tent.

"I'll eat after the pageant," Reggie said.

"No, you will not. You'll eat something now, or I'm going to kick you out," I retorted.

"You wouldn't."

"Try me," I said and crossed my arms over my chest. "You said yourself that this is my festival, and I won't allow pageant contestants that starve themselves to win."

She looked like she was about to protest again, but instead swooned a little. "Fine, I guess it wouldn't hurt to have something to eat."

"That's the spirit! We'll get a snack, and then we'll use that energy to get your things. Sound like a plan?"

"Let's do this," Reggie said right as her stomach growled like a bear.

"Any idea what you want?" I asked.

"I mean, honestly... at this point, I'd eat just about anything. You're serious that nothing will make me bloated?"

"I'm serious, but if you're worried about it, there's an exotic fruit vendor. We could get some exotic fruit salad."

Reggie thought about it for a moment and then laughed hysterically. "I'm sorry. I know that's what we should get, but no. What I really want is pancakes. Is anybody selling pancakes?"

"I think I saw pancake and sausage on a stick at the corndog vendor," I said.

"Oh, yeah. That's the ticket."

We closed the curtain on Reggie's dressing area and headed out of the pageant tent. As we walked past the exotic fruit stand, I decided that even if Reggie didn't want a salad, I was going to get one at some point. The glistening bowls of chopped fruit looked incredible.

Chapter Five

After ordering our pancakes and sausage on a stick, we stood off to the side to eat them. I only got one because I'd just had something to eat, but Reggie got two.

"What? It's one for each hand," she said when I looked shocked.

"I'm not judging you. I just think it's funny because you said you didn't want to eat."

She took a huge bite, chewed it up, and then spoke. "When Jeremy brings the boys later, I'm going to have to have them try these. They taste... magical."

"You're bringing your kids?" I asked before taking a bite of mine.

"Yeah, I hope that's okay. I just figured Jeremy could bring them for some games and we could eat dinner here. I'm always up for not cooking."

I shrugged. "I'm sure it's fine. The girls are coming for a while after school. I just imagine most kids need to be out of here by the time the sun goes down. Things will get... interesting after that."

"You mean naked," Reggie said before finishing off her right-hand pancake on a stick.

"Well, yeah. I guess that, but not like *that*."

"It's fine. We were planning on leaving after dinner. The boys will be too tired to stay late after being at school and daycare all day, and I'm sure Jeremy will need some downtime because of the murder thing."

"I'll probably have my parents take the girls so Thorn can get some rest," I said.

"He's not staying here with you?" Reggie asked.

"Not his scene," I answered. "I mean, he can if he wants to. I've got the world's most glampious glamping tent set up for me. Maybe after he gets off work, he'll decide to stay. If he wants to go home and sleep in our bed, I won't be mad at him."

"I bet he'll stay. I can't see him leaving you here alone with all these crazy witches. Especially if Brighton and Remy aren't staying."

"I think Lilith is," I said. "I'm pretty sure she reserved the tent next to mine."

"Oh, well, then he'll definitely stay. The two of you need a babysitter."

I was just about to say that Lilith and I didn't need a babysitter when a nearby conversation caught my attention.

Two witches stood in front of the Midnight Margarita stand that served margaritas at all hours, not just at midnight. They were stirring two fishbowl-sized margaritas on the rocks and talking loudly about the body. My guess was it wasn't their first margarita of the morning.

"I did see it," the one wearing a red lace maxi dress said before taking a huge gulp of her margarita. "I couldn't believe they brought stuff like that to a festival like this. I mean, all magic has its place, but this is supposed to be a festival of light. What were they thinking?"

"But do you think they did it?" The one wearing cut-off jean shorts and a tie-dye tank top asked. "I thought they were kinda creepy looking, and that's coming from me."

"Excuse me," I said as I stepped up to them and butted into their conversation. "What stuff did they bring? And why do you think it had something to do with the man's murder?"

Both women turned to me and looked stricken. I'd thought there was a chance they were trying to be overheard, but apparently, they were just buzzed and didn't realize how loudly they were speaking.

"Oh, it's, uh... you," Red Maxi Dress said.

"Clara," Tie-Dye said. "Don't say it like that."

"Lilura, I didn't mean to," Clara said and then turned to me. "I'm so sorry, Mrs. Wilson. You just caught me off guard."

"It's okay, Clara, and call me Kinsley," I said with a reassuring smile. "None of this Mrs. Wilson stuff. I'm not your high school principal."

That made Lilura laugh. "We're sorry for interrupting your breakfast. I guess we hit the booze a little early, but this is our only vacation this year."

"It's okay," I said again. "I'm glad you ladies are having fun, but I would like to know a little bit more about what you were gossiping about. Who were these witches and what did you see them bringing to the festival?"

"I guess we should have come to you sooner, but at the time we just thought they were being weird," Clara said. "It takes all kinds, you know. We didn't think anybody here might be dangerous."

"What did they have that was dangerous?"

"I mean, everything here could be dangerous," Lilura added. "but they had stuff for dark rituals. Black knives..."

"Like the one in the victim?" I interrupted.

"Yeah," Clara said. "And graveyard dirt too. Oh, and a box full of strange-looking potions."

"Strange looking how?" I pressed.

"Just... wrong. I don't know. It's hard to describe because it was a feeling that came off of everything."

"The vials were filled with black potions. Some with black smoke. And I know that's not entirely weird on its own, but I caught a good glimpse of them, and they seemed to be alive. Like they might not really be potions but something scary being contained," Lilura said.

"Held prisoner," Clara corrected.

"What did these witches look like? What kind of car were they removing these items from?" I asked.

"Well, they were dressed in all black. One wore pants and a tank top, and the other was dressed in this lacy, ankle-length dress with a white collar," Clara said.

"And they had the black lipstick and white face makeup. All of it. The whole shebang," Lilura added. "They were getting out of a red Honda. The car was quite cheerful in comparison to its owners."

"Oh, and spider earrings. Those were super cute... I mean I guess given where we are, they weren't dressed all that strangely," Clara said.

"Yeah," Lilura continued, "I think we've all got clothes like that, and I do want to get a pair of those spider earrings."

"I know I wear my share of black," I confirmed.

"But it just seemed unusual at this festival. Not the right season," Clara said.

"But some people just are who they are. We weren't judging, we swear. They just stuck out is all. And the tools they had... I mean... this just isn't the right time for shadow work," Lilura said. "Is it?"

"No, you're right. Beltane is our celebration of emerging from winter's dark. The theme of this festival is fire and flowers, so I can see why you thought it was unusual," I said and tapped my chin with my index finger. "If it was them, and I can't say whether it was or not, they were definitely sending a message."

"But who were they sending that message to?" Clara posited. "And what kind of message was a blood ritual?"

"A blood ritual…" I said as the pieces connected in my head. "I hadn't realized that's what it was."

"Lilith probably would have known right away," Reggie jumped into the conversation.

"Yeah, and she'd be positively mortified that I didn't identify it immediately," I said sheepishly. "Okay, I'm going to give you ladies my number. If you see those women again, or see anything else suspicious, call me right away."

"Yes, ma'am," they said in unison.

"And don't call me ma'am," I said with a chuckle. "Oh, and drink some water too."

Clara and Lilura nodded, and Reggie and I made our exit.

"Where are we going?" Reggie asked as I we hurried off across the festival grounds.

"To your car to get your stuff," I said.

Reggie had parked close to me in the VIP area, but I could see the regular parking area from her car. I scanned the cars as I helped her pull cases and a rolling suitcase from her trunk.

"You don't need all of this to make you beautiful," I said as I tried to pull the suitcase across the grass.

"You don't have to help me if you don't want to," she said. "I can just make two trips."

"That's not what I meant," I said. "Sorry, I'm just..."

"You're just what?"

But I'd stopped talking because I'd caught sight of exactly what I'd been searching for while unpacking the car. Across the field, about five rows in, I spotted a bright red Honda.

"Let's put this stuff back in the trunk, Reggie. We'll get it in a few minutes," I said.

"What?" Reggie asked, but then her eyes followed my line of sight. "Oh! We're investigating. Forget the pageant! Yeah, let's do this."

I'd nearly forgotten how much Reggie liked snooping. Some of our best bonding moments had been over sticking our noses into a murder investigation. We were like two peas in a sleuthing pod. Sometimes, I thought she enjoyed it even more than Dorian. Which was evident given that the pageant had meant everything to her up until about five seconds ago.

"We don't have to forgo the pageant," I said with a chuckle. "Unless that's what you really want. This should only take a few minutes."

"Unless they're the killers, and something major is about to go down. We might have to fight them," she said eagerly. "We might have to take them *down*."

That made me laugh heartily. "Reggie, please don't forget that you're surrounded by witches, and while I'd destroy anybody who hurt you, you don't actually have the magic to fend off an attack yourself. None of these witches are going fight with fists."

"Oh, right," she said and bit her bottom lip. "Well, I'll offer moral support while you fight them."

"We're not fighting anyone, Reggie," I said as I jammed the suitcase on wheels back into her trunk. "We're just talking. There's no way it's going to be that easy. We're not going to just walk over there, take their confession, and then hand them over to Thorn and Jeremy."

"That sure would be nice, though, wouldn't it?"

"And be able to just go on with the festival without this hanging over our heads? Yep, but don't count on it."

The two witches I wanted to interrogate... talk to... were leaned against the Honda puffing on joints. I could smell the cloud around them before we reached it, and while it had the distinctively skunky smell of marijuana, there was something else too. I wasn't quite sure what it was since I'd never been much of a drug user, but it did smell magical.

But I didn't have an issue with it. Magic-laced weed was probably the mildest form of mind-altering substance used at the festival. As witches, we saw the spiritual value in ceremonial use of drugs, so it wasn't against our laws or even discouraged.

Of course, those two witches were toking up and laughing hysterically at each other's fart jokes. So much so that they didn't really notice Reggie and me approaching.

"Hey, guys," I said, and they both jumped up to attention.

"Hello," the one in the tank top said.

They didn't recognize me, and I didn't know who either of them was either. I hadn't known Clara's and Lilura's names, but I'd seen them around before. The two goth witches smoking dope and talking about farts before me were complete strangers. Most likely out-of-towners in for the festival.

"Did you want to buy some weed?" the one in the dress asked.

So that explained why they were leaning against their car getting high. They were entrepreneurs. Most likely, they hadn't come to the festival to celebrate, but instead had seen a cash cow opportunity selling magic-laced weed to people as they arrived. I could respect that.

Unless they were also killers...

Which probably wasn't the case at all. They were dark and spooky looking, but neither of them had an evil aura. The witches were just goofy stoners who'd dressed that way to play a part and help them sell their... I sniffed the air again... weed laced with belladonna.

"Don't sell any of that to non-witches," I said sternly.

"Wouldn't dream of it," Tank Top said. "Are there even going to be non-witches here?"

"I'm one," Reggie said. "But I don't smoke dope, so that's not a problem for me."

Lace Dress scuffed the toe of her black pointy boot against the grass. "Are you, like, a supervisor or something?"

"I'm Kinsley Wilson formerly Skeenbauer," I said, and I saw an immediate shift in the witches' demeanor. "I'm the festival organizer as well as the head of the Skeenbauer Coven. You could say I'm the head witch around here."

"I'm sorry," tank top said. "We didn't mean to be jerks, and we would have gotten a booth, but we just didn't…"

"There's no need to lie," I cut her off. "I don't care if the two of you sell weed in the parking lot, and I don't care that it's laced with belladonna and magic as long as you don't kill any humans with it."

"Okay, thanks," lace dress said.

"What are your names?" I asked as casually as I could. I didn't want to sound like a principal taking these two witches to task. Especially if I wanted them to open up to me about the other 'stuff' they'd brought to the festival.

"I'm Nina, and this is Wren. Nina and Wren Kane. Nice to meet you, Kinsley Wilson, and?" Tank Top asked and turned toward Reggie.

"I'm Reggie. I'm Kinsley's best friend and business partner," she said proudly.

"You say you're not a witch, but I can sense a great deal of magic around you," Wren said.

"She's had a lot of spell work bestowed on her," I said quickly. "One of the perks of being best friends with a witch."

"Would be interesting if she tapped into all that power around her and learned to use it herself," Nina said.

"I can do that?" Reggie asked. "I could... tap into this magic?"

"Not now," I said and felt a pang of guilt.

I probably should have told her that at some point, but that wasn't the way. We didn't seek to convert. If someone had the ability to tap into the magic available in the world, it was on them to discover that and do it. But it was Reggie. I should have let her in on the secret, and if there had been a karmic price for doing so, I should have paid it.

There had even been a few times that Reggie had gotten so close to discovering that secret, but the veil had made her forget it. Since it was the way of things, I'd let it happen.

But it really wasn't the time. We could work it out later.

"We'll talk about it soon," I promised Reggie when she looked absolutely deflated. "I promise."

"You never told me…" she practically whispered.

"I couldn't, but the Universe has chosen this Beltane to reveal it to you, so I promise you that I'll do everything I can to help you," I said solemnly.

"You will?!" she bounced up and down, her hurt and betrayal completely evaporated by excitement.

"Of course," I said and put a hand on her shoulder. "But the two of you. Since you've brought up magic, I'd like to have a little chat about that."

"What do you mean?" Nina asked too quickly. I saw concern flash through her eyes, and I knew that she knew that I knew.

"The reason we came over here to talk to you was because someone told us they saw you unloading some concerning things from your vehicle. And as you both probably know, we had a murder occur on the festival grounds this morning. A man was killed during an unsanctioned blood ritual."

"Wedidn'thaveanythingtodowiththat," Wren garbled out.

But instantly both of them looked stone-cold sober. They dropped their joints on the ground and stubbed them out with their boots.

"You didn't have to do that," I said calmly.

"It's fine, we have plenty," Wren said, and Nina backhanded her in the gut.

"You talk too much," Nina said.

"No, that's good," I encouraged. "Trust me, ladies, it's better if you just tell me the truth right out of the gate. If you lie to me, or if Goddess help you, you hurt somebody at my festival, I'm not afraid to use the old ways."

Nina's and Wren's eyes went as wide as saucers. I saw the understanding pass between them, and they knew that my friendly demeanor was not softness. I wasn't a witch to be trifled with.

Lilith would be proud.

"We didn't kill him, if that's what you're trying to say," Nina said.

"Yeah, we were here when it happened," Wren added, and Nina elbowed her.

"How do you know when it happened?" I asked. "I don't even know exactly when it happened."

"Because we dropped those boxes off and then came right back here," Wren said.

"Oh, come on, Wren. You need to shut up," Nina said.

"No, she doesn't need to shut up, Nina. What you need to do is start talking. It's obvious you know something."

"I don't," Nina said and put her hands up in a placating gesture. "That's why she needs to shut up. We don't know anything."

"Yeah, we just did it for the cash and weed. We don't mess around with magic like that," Wren said, and Nina rolled her eyes so hard I'm sure it hurt.

"Fine," Nina relented. "I don't want to get put in a jar or turned into a goat."

"So, you do know my family's work," I said with a warning smile.

"Look, I know who you are now. We've heard of you. Everybody has heard of you, but I'd never seen you before. Sorry, but I'm not like a fangirl or anything," Nina said. "But we know better than to mess with you guys. We were just trying to make some money. She said if we delivered the boxes to the festival grounds, we'd get paid."

"And we did," Wren interrupted. "She left the weed and the cash right where she said she would. There's no way we'd ever be able to smoke that much ourselves before it went stale, so we figured we'd make some more cash. But you can see we tried it first. It's safe."

"That's really not what I care about, but I'm glad it's not poisoned. Well, I guess it is poisoned, but fine for us," I said and trailed off. "Anyway... who is this 'she' you're talking about? Who wanted you to bring the black magic stuff to the grounds? Because you guys realized she probably killed somebody."

"We don't know," Wren said.

"We met her at the gas station," Nina added. "She asked us to bring the stuff here and gave us money. Said there would be more once we did the job, and there was."

"Well, what did she look like? Did you get a name?" I demanded.

"No name," Nina said as Wren appeared to shrink into herself. The realization of what they'd done finally settling over them. "We didn't ask for a name because we're broke, and we just wanted the money. We're idiots, and apparently, it was obvious."

"What did she look like?" I asked again.

"Doesn't matter," Nina said. "We saw her, but she was using glamor magic that was obvious even to our dumbasses. At the time, it didn't occur to me that she was doing that so we couldn't identify a killer."

"Is there anything you can tell me about her?" I asked.

They thought about it for a few seconds before Wren piped up. "She was driving an old pickup truck. One of those like farmers use with the wood fence-looking things extending up out of the bed. It was old and brown with some rust around the quarter panels. Oh, and blue side mirrors. Like they'd come from another truck."

"But was she using a glamor on the truck?" I asked. "Did you pick up on that?"

"I don't know," Nina admitted. "I mean, she was by the truck the entire time we were unloading stuff, so I really couldn't tell you if the glamor magic was just on her or the truck too. Like I said, we're dumbasses. We spend too much time smoking weed and coming up with schemes."

"Now who's talking too much?" Wren said dryly.

"Do you want to get turned into a goat?" Nina sniped. "Or end up in a fancy jar decorating this witch's mantel?"

"It probably wouldn't be a fancy jar," I said dryly. "And we reserve our mantels for family. Your jar would probably end up in a cardboard box on a shelf in my basement... or garage. So is there anything else you witches need to tell me?"

They were both wearing white makeup, but even with that, I saw them go pale underneath it. Wren and Nina swallowed hard and looked at each other before looking back at me.

"We think we know him, the dead guy," Nina finally admitted. "Not personally, but we know who he is."

It occurred to me then that I hadn't given much thought to the actual identity of the victim. He'd seemed vaguely familiar. Someone I'd seen around town but didn't know personally. I'd been so wrapped up in everything else that I didn't even ask Thorn if they'd identified the guy.

"We got the munchies a while ago, and we went into the festival to get cheese on a stick. You know, like a corn dog but with cheese inside?"

"I love those," I said and put my hands on my hips. "But what does that have to do with anything?"

"We were leaving when you found the body. We saw you earlier, but we didn't know who you were then. Anyway, we got a look at the guy before we hurried back out here," Wren said.

"We thought about leaving, but then we got high again. And we thought we'd stick around for a while longer and sell some more of the weed. It's not like we'll be able to sell much of it back home. It's a good business opportunity," Nina said with a shrug.

"Okay, so you saw the guy," I said and shook my head in exasperation. "Who was he?"

"Oh, right," Nina bit her bottom lip. "Okay, so his name is… was Torin Rathmore."

"Am I supposed to know who that is?" I asked because Nina acted like that name would've cleared everything up.

"I suppose not," she admitted. "He's a goth influencer."

"A what?"

"He's an influencer," Wren said. "You know what that is, right?"

"He's on social media," I said deadpan.

"Yes, he's on all of them as a goth influencer. He did makeup tutorials, shopping hauls, graveyard tours, and paranormal investigations," Wren said. "Those were my favorite."

"Okay," I said. "Not unusual around here. Not at all."

"Yeah, except that he was a real vampire," Nina answered.

"Oh."

"Yeah."

"Oh."

Chapter Six

We left the stoner sisters to their pot smoking and selling after that and went back to Reggie's car.

"So, some witch performed a blood ritual on a vampire in the middle of your festival?" Reggie asked as we hauled her stuff to the pageant tent.

"Seems that way," I answered.

"Why would they do that?"

"To subvert the light energy of the festival for their own evil gains," I said with a shrug. "What those ends are, I don't know. But I've got to figure it out before they do it."

"Oh," Reggie answered.

"And of course, they used a vampire for their blood ritual because vampire blood is the most powerful you can get."

"Oh."

"Yeah."

"Maybe you should call off the pageant," Reggie offered.

"Maybe I should shut down the whole festival," I answered.

"You can't do that, Kinsley. If you shut everything down, then the killer will know for sure you know. They might push their plans up and create an even bigger disaster, right?"

She was right. "I guess, but how can I just keep going with this hanging over our heads? I should shut it all down and send everyone home for their own safety."

"Except that it wouldn't do any good. Those of us in Coventry wouldn't be safe."

"The town's magic would protect us," I said.

"Then it can protect us here," Reggie affirmed. "The ley line that runs under the town runs under these festival grounds. If you keep quiet about this, you get more time to investigate and more time to catch this witch while she thinks she's operating under your nose."

Reggie had a point again.

"But she is operating under my nose, Reggie. I still don't know why she did it, what she intends to do with that vampire blood, and when she intends to do it."

"Then we'll figure it out," Reggie said. "The pageant is in a little while, and hopefully, lots of people will gather to attend it. If they do, you'll be able to look around and see who's not."

"That's good thinking, but I wanted to be there to watch. To support you, Reggie."

"You don't need to watch the whole thing to support me," she said with a smile. "I'll totally forgive you if you're not standing at the stage waiting with bated breath for me to walk out in my gown or my swimsuit."

"There's a swimsuit portion?" I asked dryly.

"Yes, and don't get started on it. I know it's not feminist or whatever, but it's a spring festival, Kinsley. It's fun. The sun is shining, and I bought a killer bikini. I look so good in it."

"Killer bikini, eh?"

"Okay, bad choice of words. Just worry about the murder, and I'll let you know if I see anything hinky when I'm on stage. I'll have a pretty good view."

"Let me do your hair and makeup first?" I asked.

"Really?"

"Yes, can I?"

"I'd be honored," Reggie said with a smile so big it must have hurt.

Once I was done with her hair and makeup, Reggie shooed me out of the pageant tent to start my investigation. Since I had a few minutes, and people were still gathering, I went to go check out the crime scene.

I knew Thorn wanted everyone to stay away, but I had to get another look. Plus, I wanted to know if they'd be leaving soon. I was so torn between wishing they'd get lost so we could move on with the festival and wondering if we should...

What did all of those witches think of me that someone had the gall to do an unsanctioned blood ritual at the opening of my festival? Not that I ever would have sanctioned one in Coventry anyway.

Lilith had her shadow work, and I didn't even mind that she was teaching Hekate her ways but torturing someone like that for power... that wouldn't stand in my town. I thought that perhaps I should just shut it all down. I could send a real message that way.

But I remembered what Reggie had said. If the witches who'd performed the ritual thought they were getting away with it, then I could keep investigating. I could smoke them out like rats.

Okay, perhaps not rats. There were quite a few of them at the festival as familiars. They were both intelligent and sweet creatures even if they did have an insatiable appetite for snacks.

But who didn't, right?

I approached the crime scene tape and saw Thorn and Jeremy conversing on the other side of the scene. I'd been moving toward them at a full-on march, but I slowed my pace considerably.

While I'll spare you the gory details of the murder, I will tell you that I pulled my phone out of my pocket and took pictures as I made my way over to my husband and Jeremy.

"What are you doing?" Thorn asked as I flipped my phone closed and slid it back into my pocket.

"Taking pictures of the body," I said with a shrug. "I'll spare you the trouble of invading the crime scene in front of your other deputies or the coroner, but, Thorn, I want to take a look at the scene."

"Well, thanks… I guess," he said with a nervous laugh.

"You're most welcome. So when are you guys going to be out of here?"

"The coroner is wrapping up now," Jeremy answered. "He's taking possession of the body but because of a mass casualty event in the city, he's going to have to store the deceased at the local funeral home. He'll do the autopsy in the morning, and then the family is coming to claim the body."

"That's already been arranged?" I asked. "How?"

"The family has already been notified," Thorn said. "As far as how they pushed the autopsy to tomorrow morning and staked a claim over the body, I've been told that's above my pay grade."

"By the coroner?"

"Yeah," Jeremy said with a sigh. "First time he ever said anything like that to us. Seems that we've got some sort of VIP here."

"The guy is from Coventry," I protested. "It's not like he's a rock star or some sort of foreign diplomat." Were social media influencers really that famous?

"That we know of," Thorn answered. "I mean, he lived in Coventry. Maybe he wasn't *from* Coventry."

"I want to talk to the coroner," I said.

"Won't do you any good. If he won't tell me anything, he's not going to tell you."

"I have my ways."

"Kinsley," Thorn warned.

"Fine," I relented. "I don't need him to tell me anyway. I'll figure it out on my own."

Thorn and Jeremy both breathed a sigh of relief. "Thank you for not turning this into the kind of incident with an elected official that will land us on the international news," Jeremy said.

"I never said I wouldn't," I teased, but I also meant it. I hadn't made that promise. Nor would I. Because while I wasn't going to bother the coroner just then, that didn't mean I wouldn't have any kind of run-in with him later.

"Kinsley…" Thorn began again.

But I cut him off. "You keep saying my name like you're trying to summon me, Thorn. I'm right here."

That made him laugh, and I saw a familiar twinkle in his eyes. At one time, Thorn thought he wanted a nice quiet life with a good, well-behaved wife. Turned out, he didn't know what the heck he wanted. As much as he protested, my newfound embrace of my magic, and my take-charge attitude, got his motor running.

I winked at him and then wandered off a few feet to scroll through the pictures. I didn't want to go far in case I saw something. If I did, I'd risk the coroner seeing me poking around the scene. Plus, I wanted to be close to Thorn in case I had questions or needed to bring something to his attention.

The thing that stuck out to me the most in the photos, other than the black ceremonial knife sticking out of the victim's chest, was the locket around his neck. It was a rose gold locket with a crescent moon in the center. The moon was composed of diamonds, and immediately, it did not strike me as a man's necklace. Men could wear what they wanted, but it did not match his attire at all. To be fair, he only wore tight leather pants and black motorcycle boots. But his skin also bore a tapestry of tattoos and the man, Torin Rathmore, had a few piercings as well.

I had to wonder if he knew Azriel. Wow, that was a name I hadn't thought about for a long time. Azriel had been my husband for one day. He was my vampire lover who I nearly chose over Thorn at one point, but he tried to have me killed for money. That kind of put a damper on our "true love."

Lilith still hadn't forgiven me for choosing Thorn over Azriel. "What's a little attempted murder when you've got a hot biker vampire like that?" she'd ask from time to time. "Have you seen the butt on that guy? His biceps? I'd let him murder me every day of the week and twice on Sundays."

I'd told her she should marry him then. She said she'd considered it...

Anyway...

Jeremy and Thorn were huddled together talking when I inched closer to the body. I knew that I probably shouldn't do it, but I wanted to see inside the locket. With a subtle flick of my fingers, I opened it, took a photo, and then with another artful move of my hand, I closed it again and walked off.

Once I was on lost in the crowd again, I opened the photo on my phone and zoomed in. I wasn't quite sure what I would find inside, but my discovery wasn't completely surprising. The photo was of the victim.

I supposed it was strange that the man was wearing a locket with a photo of himself, but I deduced that at one point, it must have been a gift for someone else. For whatever reason, it was back in his possession, and he wore it too.

That sounded like a gift for a woman, and its return was probably not a happy occasion. A breakup? One that Torin hadn't gotten over. Or perhaps the woman he loved had died. I had no way of knowing unless I dug deeper into his life.

The coroner began to load the body into a bag to put in his van. As he did, a hush fell over the crowd. The pageant was beginning.

I patrolled the perimeter. I didn't have a good view into the middle of the crowd, but I figured anyone up to no good would be around the periphery.

But nothing happened. People all around me seemed to be having a good time watching the pageant. Those who weren't ate food, played games, or did perfectly safe and sanctioned magic.

It felt weird to me that people had moved on so quickly after Torin's death, but it was relief too. If darkness and sadness had taken hold of everyone, or even most people, the evil witches who'd taken a man's life would have tons of black energy to feed from.

So, I drifted back toward the stage because I didn't want to miss Reggie's parts of the pageant. I ended up standing right next to Jeremy, who had his phone out and ready to take video to show the kids.

"The boys will get a kick out of this," he said with a smile. "Everything but the swimsuit competition. Reggie begged me not to record that even though we go swimming all of the time together."

"It's different when she's up on stage, in heels, strutting her stuff," I said.

"I suppose," Jeremy agreed. "They'll love the rest of it, though. The boys will be so proud of their mother, and I'm proud of her too... for doing this. It took a lot."

"Reggie has always been brave," I said. "But don't you have a murder investigation? I can record this for you."

"Are you kidding? I wouldn't miss this for the world. If Thorn hadn't given me a couple of hours off to watch, I'd have resigned."

I couldn't help but smile. Jeremy was like a brother to me, and he was such a good man. The pride and love in his eyes waiting for Reggie to come out on stage was staggering.

"Well, I guess it's a good thing Thorn has a good head on his shoulders."

I'll spare you the details of the pageant. But much to my shock, and the utter surprise of the crowd, Reggie won. It was too bad Jeremy had to leave before they announced the Flower Queen. He'd stayed long enough to take video of her competing, but neither one of us thought she was going to win.

Fortunately, when she made the final round, I started filming the crowning ceremony. Dorian had joined me as well, and I swear when they announced the runner-up, and it became obvious that Reggie was the new Flower Queen,

Dorian screamed so loud it nearly broke my eardrum.

Once they put the crown she won on her head and handed her the flowers, Reggie ran down the stage steps and jumped into our arms.

Chapters Seven

"I've got to tell you something," Reggie said once she and Dorian stopped ugly crying. And I fixed her makeup...

"You can say I told you so all you want. I'll probably never live this down, but let those witches talk. I'm so happy for you," I said.

"Not about that," Reggie's face looked suddenly serious.

"What is it? What's wrong?"

"I saw something when I was on stage. It was during the swimsuit portion."

"What did you see?" I asked.

"There was a woman in the crowd acting strangely," Reggie answered.

"What do you mean by strangely?"

"Well, for one thing, she was dressed in a red trench coat and a huge floppy black hat. Her attire stuck out like a sore thumb."

"That does sound a little weird, but I'm not sure if the killer would want to make themselves more noticeable."

"That's true," Reggie said and bit her bottom lip. "You're right. Besides all of the witches seem to have their own style. Forget I brought it up."

"No, we shouldn't just dismiss it. Something about her made you suspicious, and we really don't have any other leads. I think we should look into it. Perhaps she was hiding in plain sight. Maybe she knew we'd think the killer wouldn't dress in such an obvious manner, so what better disguise."

"You think?"

"I do," I said. "Why don't you get changed quickly, and we'll take a look around for her."

"Get changed? Are you crazy? I'm wearing this gown until I go to bed. The crown too. Heck, I'll probably wear the crown until it falls apart. I'm not taking it off."

I just looked at her for a moment. Reggie was completely serious.

"Okay," I said. "But let me know if you get uncomfortable."

"I get to come too, right?" Dorian asked.

"What would we do without you?" I countered.

"Good point."

"So, Reggie, you said she was wearing a red coat and a huge black hat?"

"Yep," she confirmed.

"All right, that shouldn't be too hard to find."

"Unless she ditched them or was using a glamor," Dorian said.

"Ugh, witches," I complained.

"I can help," a voice came from between my feet.

I looked down, and Meri sat there swishing his tail lazily.

"Yes, you go survey as much of the crowd as you can. We're going to go that way," I said and pointed toward the food stands. "You go deeper and watch the witches in the 'witches only' areas. Let us know if you find anything."

"Will do," he said and darted off. Meri only got a few feet before he stopped and turned back to us. "There better be some bacon in this for me."

"You know it," I answered, and then he was gone.

Reggie, Dorian, and I made our way around looking for the woman in red. We weren't having any luck, but that might have had something to do with us stopping twice for snacks.

I could always eat, but Reggie was ready to feast since the pageant was over. Dorian sipped a coffee and nibbled on a croissant.

While I should have tried harder to keep us on task, I didn't mind hovering around the food stalls so I could keep an eye on the crime scene. By that point, the body and the deputies were gone, but I wondered if the killer would come back to relive their kill.

Had they only killed that vampire for the blood? Or was it someone who had enjoyed torturing him?

Perhaps it was both, and if it was, I was sure they would come back to try to get another thrill out of the murder. I was so engrossed in watching people circle around the former scene that I didn't hear or see Meri approach.

I nearly jumped halfway out of my skin when he said, "Found her!" from between my feet.

"Oh, Goddess, you startled me," I said with my hand pressed high on my chest.

"Maybe you should buy some pot from those weirdos in the parking lot," Meri snarked.

"I need to stay sharp," I countered.

"Saying that you need to stay sharp is assuming you were ever sharp in the first place," he said and took off.

"Come on, guys," I turned and said to Reggie and Dorian. "Meri said he found the woman, and he just ran off."

Without waiting for their response, I started running after Meri. He darted around most people, but a few times, he ran between their feet. One witch almost fell.

Just like a cat... I thought as I pursued him.

Eventually, we crossed through an area cordoned off with red ropes. If you looked closely enough at the brass poles holding up the ropes, you'd see tiny sigils carved in the metal. It was a VIP area for practicing more dangerous types of magic.

None of the human attendees could enter unless they had their own sigil to grant them access. Reggie and Dorian could technically come inside, but I wondered if they would. That level of magic could be overwhelming and repulsive to regular folks, especially with so much of it going on in a concentrated area.

I followed Meri and found him standing outside of a large, black tent. I could smell burning candles and a mélange of herbs coming from inside.

"Is she in there?" I asked.

Meri nodded toward a stack of boxes sitting on the opposite side of the entrance. Flopped on top was a red trench coat and huge black hat.

I pushed the curtain open and walked inside. The inside of the tent was full of shelves containing various magical items plus a wide array of candles. In the very center was a huge cauldron. A fire beneath it boiled the contents.

One peek inside revealed a simmering pool of lime-green potion. As it bubbled, though, the bubbles turned purple and floated away. Each lavender orb dissipated before it reached the tent's high ceiling.

A woman turned from the back of the tent and threw a handful of plants into the pot. She then placed a large, wooden paddles in the potion and began to stir. As she did, the contents turned burgundy like wine.

"What can I help you with?" she asked softly. "I'm brewing a love potion now, but a vial of it will cost you."

"Love potion?" I asked. "Are you sure you should be doing that?"

Her eyes lit up with recognition. "Kinsley, oh, hello. I mean..."

"No, no. It's okay. I shouldn't question you. It's just that I, and my family, we don't condone the use of love potions. But to each her own."

"I understand," the woman said. "But this potion is a special brew. It doesn't override the will of another. It will only bring out love that already exists. And, if you drink it under a new moon, it can cure heartbreak."

"Oh, that's cool," I said and stepped closer. "I just assumed, and I apologize."

"No harm done," she responded. "I'm Canary. Canary Blackwell. I'm from Minnesota."

"It's nice to meet you, Canary. Are you in here alone?" I asked as I surveyed the interior.

There weren't many places to hide, but it was a large tent. Someone could have been concealed behind a few of the shelves, but as we talked,

Meri walked around looking for our potential killer.

"It's just me," Canary answered.

"So, is that your red coat and hat outside?"

"It is," she answered. "Why?"

"You were... someone saw you during the pageant. You had the coat and hat on, and from what I understand, you seemed suspicious."

She took a deep breath. "I have a bit of a curse on me," she revealed. "I have some trouble in the sun, so I wear the coat and hat whenever I'm out of the tent. I mean, except at night. I try to stay in here during the day."

"A curse? Like the kind of thing you'd pick up doing necromancy on a vampire?" I took a harder look around and at the cauldron bubbling before me. I'd said the red looked like wine, but perhaps it was more like blood.

"Oh," Canary said. "Oh, no. Nothing like that. I see what you're getting at, but that wasn't me. I promise. Here, try some of the potion. It's not blood magic, I promise."

Canary grabbed a ladle and a crystal chalice. She scooped out some of the potion and poured it carefully into the glass.

"It's not hot," she said and thrust the glass toward me. "I promise."

I took the glass and sniffed the potion inside. It smelled of strawberries despite the fact that it probably contained none. "Meri, come here," I called out to him.

I doubted there was anything in the potion that could do me much harm, but I wanted him there just in case. If she tried to poison me, either magically or with mundane toxins, I wanted him ready to assist me with healing magic.

"My friends are on their way here," I said before examining the glass again.

"Do you think they'd want some potion?" Canary asked with genuine confusion.

"No, I just want you to know that even if you managed to overpower me with this potion, you won't have time to dispose of me before more people arrive at your tent."

"Oh, Kinsley, no. I promise, it's just a mild love potion. Try it. You'll see."

I sniffed the chalice again. As far as I could tell, there was no blood in the recipe. But before I took a sip, I knelt down and let Meri sniff it.

I wasn't very good with potions. Something else I needed to work on, of course. But since I usually didn't need them, it hadn't been a priority.

"Seems fine," Meri said. His little pink tongue darted out of his mouth and lapped up a few drops of the potion. "Tastes like strawberries."

"Meri, you didn't have to do that," I chastised. "I just wanted you to smell it."

"Get on with it," he groused. "I'm fine."

"Okay, okay," I said and stood up. "Cheers," I said to Canary before bringing the glass up to my lips.

I sipped it tentatively at first, but the taste and scent of fresh-picked strawberries overwhelmed my senses in a good way. I found myself tipping the cup up and gulping the rest of the sweet, fruity potion down. Before I could open my eyes, I swore I felt sunshine on my skin, and the fresh, green scent of growing things wafted over me.

"Oh, my gosh," I said and handed the chalice back to Canary. "That tastes amazing."

"Could you feel the sun that grew the berries?" she asked.

"I could," I said. "But there aren't any actual strawberries in there, right? That's amazing."

"It's pretty cool," she said with a shrug. "I've worked on my potions for a long time. Ever since I was a kid with a chemistry set. Except I never used it for actual chemistry."

I chuckled. "I understand. I loved mundane subjects when I was school aged, but not every witch does. So what were you doing during the pageant? I believe you about the potions, but is everything okay? Are you okay?"

"Oh, yeah, Kinsley. I was just looking for my familiar. She left the tent, and I needed her to get this batch correct. Sometimes she'd hard to keep track of, though."

"Your familiar?"

"Luluanne!" Canary called out over her shoulder. "What are you up to?" She turned back to me. "I hope she didn't take off again."

"I'm here," a little voice said from behind one of the shelves.

A few seconds later, a raccoon dressed in a pink tutu waddled out from behind one of the shelves. She sat down next to Canary's feet and looked up at me.

After looking me up and down, Luluanne turned her attention to Meri. "You're a strange-looking raccoon."

"Is she serious?" Meri asked.

"I think she is," I answered. "Don't be rude."

"Lulu thinks everyone is a raccoon," Canary said. "Well, she thinks all other familiars are."

"That's because they are," Luluanne said. "I keep trying to explain it to you, but you never listen."

"I know," Canary said. "It's better to just let her have it."

"You're not letting me have anything," Lulu said. "It's true. Do we have any grapes? I'm going to go get some grapes. I think I saw some…"

"Lulu, don't you wander off again. There are grapes in the cooler," Canary said.

"Green ones?" the raccoon asked.

"Of course."

"Well, too bad because I want black grapes."

"We've got those too," Canary said with a tinge of exasperation.

"Really? Are you sure? Because if not, I can go get more."

"Lulu, there are black grapes in the cooler. Just go get some."

"Fine, but if there aren't any red grapes, I'm going out."

"There are red too," Canary said.

And with that, Lulu waddled off toward the back of the tent. Suddenly, Meri's snark and sass didn't seem all that bad. At least I didn't have to deal with him wandering off when I needed him to look for food we already had, and he did not think that every familiar was a cat… or raccoon.

"Well, thank you for talking with me," I said. "Sorry if I came off as accusative."

"It's okay. You must be under a ton of pressure. I just wish there was something I could do to help," Canary said. "If you need any potions during the festival, maybe I could hook you up? I've got lots of obscure recipes."

"Perhaps," I said. "Or maybe there's something else. You said you have a curse on you that has something to do with vampires, right? Did you know the man that died was a vampire?"

"I promise you I had nothing to do with any of that. This is going to sound strange, but I have security cameras outside of this tent. My potions use expensive and hard-to-get ingredients, and while I've not had any trouble at this festival, I've had issues with theft before. So I can show you. I can show you that I didn't leave the tent during the time he was killed."

I thought about it for a moment. Should I ask her to show me?

Before I could say anything, Reggie and Dorian finally caught up. They walked into the tent, and Canary's eyes widened.

"How did you get in here?" she demanded.

In tandem, Reggie and Dorian held up their wrists. "We have these."

"They're my friends," I said. "I gave them sigils to let them go anywhere they want to go."

"Oh," Canary whispered.

"They're fine. I assure you they can handle being here, but I've thought it over, and I would like to see your footage."

"Footage?" Dorian asked.

"She has security footage of herself and her tent while the murder took place. I'd like to see it before we go," I said.

With a nod, Canary removed her wood paddle from the cauldron and set it aside. "Follow me."

She led us to a back section of the tent that was a separate room. Inside, Luluanne was munching on grapes, and when we walked inside, she scrambled into the cooler. I couldn't help but chuckle as she pulled the lid shut and closed herself inside with her fruit.

"Is she always like that?" I asked as Canary booted up a laptop on a folding table.

"Oh, trust me, it gets so much worse. Like when your friend saw me earlier trying to find her. At least she didn't pull any of her shenanigans while the murder was happening or else I wouldn't have my alibi."

"If you were in this tent the entire time, then how do you know when the murder happened?" Dorian asked from over my shoulder. Good old Dorian always thinking like a reporter.

"You're kidding, right?" Canary answered while she kept tapping away at the laptop's keyboard. "I've had four people in here already today talking about it. I know enough details that it's like I was there."

With that, she turned the laptop around to face me and clicked a button. The security footage began to play, and I saw the time stamp at six in the morning. Canary took the boxes that were currently out in front of the tent and set them down, and then she disappeared back into the tent.

I watched for a couple of minutes and nothing happened. I was about to ask about speeding it up when Canary spoke up.

"Fast forward is there," she said and pointed to an arrow.

I clicked it because I had no desire to stand there watching the footage for hours. One thing I did notice was that nobody came and went for the first two or so hours. She didn't leave, and nobody came in either.

Then, around the time I dispersed the crowd so Thorn and the deputies could work, people started to either walk by the tent or come in.

"You see," she said and clicked the button to stop the footage once we were well past where the murder had occurred. "I was here the whole time."

"And there's no back entrance to this tent," Dorian pressed.

"You can have a look yourself," she said and waved toward the back of the tent.

Dorian did, and when he didn't find anything, he shook his head "no."

"Well, thank you for your time and for going so far out of your way to prove your innocence," I said. "I do appreciate it."

"I'm just glad you feel that way," Canary said. "It would figure that Luluanne sneaking off for snacks would make me a murder suspect. I swear that raccoon..."

"Well, let me buy some of that potion you were brewing up front. It's the least I can do," I said.

"You don't have to," Canary protested.

"I know, but I'd like to," I said.

"I'll take some too," Dorian piped up.

"Me too," Reggie added. She'd been so quiet I'd almost forgotten she was there.

"Can I even sell it to them?" Canary asked me. "I'm not sure that's ethical."

"It's fine," I said with a wave of my hand. "You have my permission, and I take responsibility for it."

"Okay, if you insist," Canary said with a shrug. "I'm not going to turn down sales if you're fine with it."

After that, Canary filled three little crystal potion bottles with her special love brew, and then put each of them in a small paper gift bag. We all paid for our purchases, and then headed out of the tent.

While the footage and the lack of rear entrance to the tent wasn't a 100 percent alibi, I was confident that Canary didn't have anything to do with the murder. Sure, she could have used magic to fake some of what we'd seen, but I just didn't believe she had.

"Sorry about that," Reggie said. "I didn't mean to waste your time."

"You didn't," I said. "At least now we know, and we can focus our attention elsewhere."

"I would like to play some games," Dorian suggested. "If we can take a break from the murder investigation for a few minutes."

"It wouldn't really be taking a break though. It's more like surveillance. We've got to blend in, so the only way to really solve this murder is to enjoy the festival," I said.

"I like the way you think," Dorian replied.

"Shall we pop some balloons with darts?" Reggie asked. "I have my eye on a giant pink unicorn stuffie."

"Let's go," I said, and we headed off toward the carnival games.

Later that night, it was just me and Thorn. The girls had come to the festival for a visit, but they'd left with my mom and dad before it started to get too dark.

I could see in Thorn's eyes that he was debating whether he should leave or not. I knew he kind of wanted to get out of there before the skyclad naked shenanigans got started, but he also didn't really want to leave me.

Not that he didn't trust me. There was probably still a part of him that thought he should be there to protect me because there was a killer on the loose. That part of Thorn would never change, and to tell the truth, I didn't really want it to anyway. I liked that he wanted to take care of me.

"You know that there's room in my tent for two, right?" I asked with my eyebrow cocked. "And the girls are staying with my parents."

"Are you inviting me to stay?" Thorn asked softly.

"You know I want you here, Thorn. It was you who didn't believe you belonged, but I think you do. I know you think we're very different..."

But he cut me off, "I used to think that, Kinsley. Now, I'm not so sure anymore. I mean, I know I'm not a witch, but..."

"But you've always been able to see through the veil. At least partially. You were meant for my world."

"Well, when you put it like that, how could I possibly resist?" Thorn asked.

"How about some dinner?" I proposed. "I know you were supposed to leave this investigation to me, but I also know you didn't. You probably ran yourself ragged today and didn't eat properly."

"Guilty as charged," Thorn answered. "So, what's good here? What do I have to try?"

I laughed. "All of the food is good. What are you in the mood for?"

He thought about it for a second. "Pork burgers and kettle corn," Thorn finally answered.

"Oh, two of my favorites! And the stands selling those items just happened to be right next to each other."

"You're kidding, right? They really have both here?"

"Of course they do. Pork burgers and kettle corn are Illinois festival staples. And they are so good because the women making them are witches," I said with a wink.

"Lead the way," Thorn said.

We were standing in line for the pork burgers when Thorn got a look on his face. I'd known him long enough to know that it meant something big.

"What is it?" I asked as the line took a collective step forward.

"We found something on the body, and I'm not sure if I feel bad for not mentioning it sooner, or if I just shouldn't say anything."

"Yes, Thorn. You should say something," I insisted.

"I just don't want to send you down a rabbit hole on a wild goose chase," he answered.

"That was a lot of metaphors," I countered. "You smashed them together quite nicely, though. Interesting visual."

With that, Thorn pulled a plastic baggie out of his pocket and handed it to me. I took it and looked it over. Inside the bag was a small, white slip of paper. It took me a couple of seconds to decipher what I held in my hands.

"It's a Brew Station receipt," I said.

"Yeah, and it's from this morning. Quite early, too. Must have been right after they opened."

"Oh," I said. "He was in there when they might have been slow. Vivian might have seen him."

"It's probably nothing," Thorn said. "Lots of people get their morning coffee there. Anyway, I can just stop in there tomorrow morning and ask her about it."

Chapter Eight

But when I woke up the next morning, there was a strange buzz in the air. Thorn had already left for work, but that wasn't unusual. He'd probably slipped out of bed before four to go for a run and then home to shower.

I looked at my phone and saw that it was just after five. The sun hadn't begun its ascent into the sky yet, but there was the faintest hint of purple twilight on the horizon.

The festival grounds were practically silent. It was almost spooky in a way, because I would have expected people to be up partying until dawn.

I got dressed quickly and exited my tent. No one was around. It was like the entire festival was a ghost town, but I quickly realized that everyone was in their tents.

Not everyone was sleeping, though. As I walked around, an occasional person would part the entrance of their tent and peek out. As soon as I'd make eye contact with them, they'd quickly close the tent.

But I wasn't entirely alone. I heard a noise behind me and turned to see Meri dart out from the tent to join me. He'd been sleeping soundly when I got up, so I'd left him to sleep while I investigated.

"You left me behind," he said, but strangely, he was whispering.

"Meri, why are you whispering?"

"I don't want to wake everyone up," he said like it was obvious, and I was stupid.

"Don't you think it's a little strange that everyone is in their tents?"

"It's early," he said offhand, but then he stopped in his tracks. "Wait a minute. Why *would* everyone be sleeping?"

"That's what I'm saying," I said. "It's... spooky."

"Hey, you!" Meri said loudly, and I turned my attention to a tent that had the entrance curtain pulled open a few inches. "Hey, why are you in there watching us? Come out."

But the woman closed the tent. I heard a rustling to my left and turned to see Dorian emerging from his tent.

"Whoa," he said as he walked over to us.

"What?" I asked wanting to know what he was referring to.

"It feels weird out here, but I'm just not sure..." he started to say but then stopped and scratched the back of his neck. "It's like we're being watched."

"I get that. These witches keep peeking out of their tents," I answered.

"No, not that. Not just being watched like that."

"I don't know what you mean," I said, but I could feel it too.

"Like we're being stalked. Like we're prey," he said. "I imagine this is what a rabbit feels like right before a hawk swoops down and grabs it."

"Yeah," I agreed and took a deep, shuddering breath. "Yeah, but why?"

My biggest fear was that the witch who'd performed the blood ritual had already achieved her goal. In addition to the feeling of being watched, the air was charged with that same sensation you feel right before a bad storm hits.

But the sky was clear. I could see the remains of the stars.

I could only imagine what we were feeling was the same thing people felt right before a disaster. It was like a volcano was about to explode or... I didn't know.

And then I saw something off in the distance. Faint lights moved slowly down the road toward the festival grounds.

Dorian, Meri, and I stood there watching for what felt like hours. While everything in me wanted to cross the field between us and the lights to get a closer look, something inside of me made me stay put. I was frozen in place like a deer in headlights. And I realized that same feeling was what drove all of the witches around me into their tents.

Eventually, we could see what moved ominously in our direction. It was a caravan of sleek, black Rolls Royces. There were dozens of them practically idling down the road toward us.

"What in the heck?" I whispered.

"Should we call someone?" Dorian asked.

"Who are we going to call?" I asked.

"Oh, I don't know. Your husband maybe?"

"I don't think his department is equipped to handle whatever this is, and besides, we don't know what this is."

"I'd still feel better if there were some guns involved."

"Guns? Please, Dorian. We're surrounded by witches. The magic here is way more powerful than guns."

"Except that all of these super powerful witches are hiding in their tents," Meri groused. "And not all of them are super powerful. Some of them bake... cake... that makes people extra happy."

"You guys have a point, but I'm still not calling Thorn. I'm not putting humans in danger for whatever this is. I'll handle it," I said and pushed up the sleeves of the black cardigan I'd donned to ward away the morning chill.

Dorian and Meri hurried after me as I crossed the field toward the slow-moving line of cars. Dorian called after me. "Kinsley, there are thirteen cars! This is insane."

"It's not insane. I can handle it, but you should go back," I said over my shoulder.

"Not a chance," Dorian said in his 'serious business' voice, and he picked up his pace.

"You're all nuts," Meri said as he darted ahead of me. "But this is too good to miss."

The only thing I was glad of was that Reggie had gone home with her boys the night before. She'd sworn she was going to spend the night at the festival and live it up, but in the end, she just wanted to go home and put them to bed. I understood. Fortunately for me, my daughters were a little older, and I'd grown used to them spending the night away because they spent so much time at their grandparents' house.

Suddenly, the cars stopped.

And so did I.

The foreboding feeling that I'd been successful at ignoring up until that moment hit me like a brick wall. It took every ounce of my willpower not to turn tail and run back to my tent.

But what good would it do? I rationalized. A cloth tent was not going to stop whoever, or whatever, was in those cars.

Every driver's side door opened in sync. Men dressed in gray trench coats with black leather hats stepped out in time, and it almost looked like a dance.

Each of them swept around the backs of the cars and opened the back passenger door. As they stepped back, the cars' other occupants stepped out.

"This is a little ridiculous," Meri said.

"Shhh," I warned.

"Seriously, Kinsley? These people are what everyone one is so scared of? All of this showing off tells me they aren't really that scary. Truly scary people don't have to act like this."

"Shh," I warned again.

"Fine," he relented, but I also noted that he stepped behind me.

Scary Meri who ate demons for breakfast was even unnerved. He'd been trying to convince himself not to be afraid, not me. But he couldn't die, so what could possibly rattle him to such a degree?

There were thirteen men standing next to their Rolls Royces as their drivers practically floated back around the cars and disappeared inside. I couldn't focus on all of them at once, so I studied the one in the middle.

I was still so far away, so I tried to take a step closer. Dorian's hand shot out and grabbed me around the wrist.

"Dorian, come on. It's obvious they are here to talk, so let's go meet them," I tried to sound braver than I felt.

"I don't think they are here to talk," he answered.

The men began moving toward us. I would say walking, but that wasn't exactly the effect. It was as if they were gliding. The one in the middle who I'd tried to focus on took the lead, and the rest followed him in a V formation like a flock of geese.

As he moved closer, I got a better look. His long black hair hung thick and lustrous, but completely straight, nearly down to his waist. He wore a white cotton shirt that tucked into pants that could only be described as breaches. All of them were dressed the same too. Over their shirts and tight pants were red velvet jackets. Their feet were shoed in black boots.

For a moment, I started to think it was a joke. They looked like extras from a cheesy teen vampire movie. I half expected their skin to sparkle when the sun finally rose.

But that moment of levity ended abruptly when I saw their eyes. I'd met vampires before, but none of them had such black pits for irises. Their predatory gazes made me swallow back a yelp.

These men were vampires, but they weren't just any vampires. Their skin was so white and smooth looking that if they weren't moving, I'd have assumed they were carved out of marble. I could feel the cold emanating off of them. It was that same chilly feeling you get when you stand inside a mausoleum. Cold and hard like stone even on the warmest summer day.

"Dorian, go back to the festival," I instructed after swallowing the terrified lump in my throat.

"He should stay," the third man back said.

My eyes flicked to him. He looked like a carbon copy of the dark god standing before me, except that his hair was flaxen, and he had some sort of blue gem affixed to his lapel.

The one in front of me stooped to pick up Meri. It happened in a flicker of movement. One moment he was empty-handed, and the next his white hands held my familiar.

Meri struggled for a moment, but the vampire let out a shush that was mostly a hiss of quiet breath. Meri stilled, but he looked at me with wide, startled eyes.

"Don't hurt him," I warned.

"And what would you do?" The vampire asked with one side of his full lips quirked up in a half smile.

"It would do you good not to find out," I countered. The sight of a frightened Meri helped me find my backbone.

These men were predators, and everything about them was intended to trick you into freezing in fright. They wanted me to be scared because that made their job easier.

But what they didn't know was that I was the thing to truly be afraid of... even if I didn't always remember that.

"Put him down," I demanded, and a clap of thunder rang out overhead.

"Fine," the vampire said and released Meri. "But be careful, witch."

"I think it's you who needs to be careful, sir. Coming here with your fancy little show, and then putting your hands on my familiar. Without his or my permission, I might add. What is the meaning of this spectacle?"

"First, an introduction," The vampire said and extended a long, slender hand to me. "Don't worry, I don't bite."

That made his twelve companions erupt in laughter. But it lasted mere seconds, and then complete, dead silence descended around us again.

I took his hand because I had to prove I was not afraid. His skin was as smooth and cold as marble, but from somewhere inside of him, I felt a deep, pulsing vein of ancient energy. No, these were not mere vampires. They were ancient and powerful.

But so was the magic that ran through me.

"I'm Kinsley Wilson," I said and then added, "of the Skeenbauer Coven. Now, who are you? And what is the meaning of all of this?"

But a slick feeling of sickness threatened my stomach. We'd had a vampire murdered during a blood ritual, and now these guys had rolled up to Coventry. Whatever they wanted, it wasn't good.

Chapter Nine

"Can we go somewhere a little more comfortable?" Lothaire asked.

That was his name, by the way. He finally finished the introduction part of the conversation and then moved on to being horrified by the festival accommodations.

"Don't you have an old castle or even an abandoned cathedral?" Lothaire asked as we stood outside Craft Donuts.

I'd tried to get them to settle on a large tent at the festival but to no avail. My employees at Craft Donuts stared out the window at us in horror.

"Don't I wish," I said with a chuckle, but the vampires did not find it funny.

"What about that establishment?" Lothaire asked and pointed at the Brew Station.

"All right," I said and led them inside.

Fortunately, the vampires' presence scared off the few early morning customers. To make up for it, I ordered a hundred dollars' worth of fancy coffee drinks and pastries for my new friends.

"What's going on?" Viv asked as she eyed her new customers with caution.

"I'm not sure. They arrived at the festival in a slow-moving line of Rolls Royces and then confronted me in the middle of the field. They haven't told me what they want yet. They insisted on going somewhere more comfortable, and they seemed to like your shop," I said. "Not big on donuts, I guess."

"That's too bad," Viv said with a shake of her head. "I guess I should be flattered, though."

"They really seem to like the pastries despite being vampires," I observed. "And the coffee."

"Are they going to kill us all?" Viv got right to the point.

"I can't say that's not their intention, but Viv, I won't let that happen."

"I trust you," she said. "I'll keep the lattes flowing."

"Thank you."

Viv handed me my favorite hazelnut latte, and I made my way back over to the table to join

Lothaire. "Is this comfortable enough? Could you please tell me what you, and your gentlemen friends, are doing in Coventry?"

"My brother is dead," Lothaire said before taking a sip of his coffee.

Oh, no.

"So, you understand?" Lothaire asked between swallows.

"I'm sorry about your brother."

"I didn't come here for an apology," his voice had a razor's edge.

The breath I didn't know I was holding escaped my lips as a startled hiss. "I don't..."

He cut me off. "That gathering we came from was all witches, correct?"

"It was," I answered dutifully.

"And one of them killed my brother during some sort of sacrifice?"

"A blood ritual, but it wasn't sanctioned. I can assure you that."

"I believe you, Kinsley Wilson, or we wouldn't be having this conversation. I'd have... dealt with you already."

"Then what do you want?" I practically whispered.

"So crass," Lothaire chastised. "So crass, but direct. I suppose that's good."

I nodded my head, willing the whole thing to be over.

"What I want is the witch who did it."

"I will find her," I responded. "And I…"

"No!" Lothaire slapped the table. His eyes gleamed with malice. "You will find her, and then you will hand her over to me. There is no other way."

Viv came out from behind the counter and started toward me. Her human instincts to protect her friend were stronger than the one for self-preservation. My eyes widened and I jerked my head to indicate she should retreat.

But Lothaire spoke first. "Ah, another coffee. That would be wonderful," he said to Viv.

The malice was gone from his eyes, and his face bore his welcoming smile. But I knew it was all fake, his expression perfectly crafted to pull in prey.

"Who are you?" I asked.

I didn't agree to turn the witch who killed Torin over to the vampires, but I didn't need to. I really had no other choice. While Lothaire's conclave of vampires couldn't destroy me or Coventry, I knew they could do some damage. And there was a fire behind his eyes that let me know he'd endure whatever pain I could throw at him to exact his price on Coventry.

I didn't even know if the witch who killed Torin was from Coventry, but we would pay for her transgressions. In fact, I seriously doubted it was a Coventry witch. It was some wicked outsider who had used my festival as a cover. A fire, like the one in Lothaire's eyes, began to burn in my belly.

"The human world has its laws," Lothaire began to answer my question, and his words broke into my thoughts. "Well, so do we."

"I agree. It is the same with witches, but that doesn't tell me who you are," I pressed gently.

"Just as humans have their politicians and law enforcement, so do we."

"So, you're... like the vampire police?"

"No. I decided not to send them, and I came myself. As your world has royalty,"

"We don't," I interrupted.

That made Lothaire laugh. The sound was gentle and melodic, but I knew it was another trick to pull a person... a victim... in. "Oh, Kinsley. You have no idea who you really are, do you? No matter. I know who you are, and so does everyone else. You are a beautiful, disastrous mess, but you are special."

"I'm not sure what to say to that, but I guess a thank you is in order."

His smile widened. It almost met his eyes.

"All that is to say that we vampires have what you would call royalty too. And my wayward brother was a member of that family."

"As are you," I said softly. "I didn't know."

"That's the way we like it, Kinsley. I'm glad you didn't know, but now you do. And since we are the same, I will give you three days to turn the killer over to me. After that, the matter will be mine." Lothaire stood abruptly, and so did all of his companions.

Viv and I stood at the window and watched them all sink into their respective Rolls Royces. We were awestruck by the way they all pulled out of the parking spaces and slowly drove off like a perfectly synchronized funeral procession.

All but one.

When I turned around, one of the vampires still sat at the Brew Station's last table before the hall that led to the restrooms. He smiled before taking a large bite of the cherry tart perched between his fingers like a teacup, his pinky extended and all.

"Looks like they left a babysitter," I said to Viv.

She shuddered. But before she could say anything, that remaining vampire was gone. He'd disappeared from the coffee shop in a blur.

"What was that about?" I asked.

Just then, Dorian came through the door. He'd been waiting outside in my car because I'd told him it was too dangerous for him to sit in the room full of ancient vampires with me. Viv and her staff had been in danger, but I couldn't prevent that. At least with Dorian outside, it was one less human for me to worry about.

"Dorian!" Viv exclaimed before running over to hug him.

It was obvious she was nearly hysterical with relief that the vampires were gone. Dorian held her for a moment until she was calm, and then she set off to make his favorite coffee.

Dorian crossed the room to me and held out his hand. "He gave me this," he said. "When he came out, I was getting out of the car. He just floated over to me and gave me this."

It was a pendant. A large square cut ruby surrounded by diamonds on a heavy gold chain.

"That's..." I began to say but trailed off because I sensed something about the necklace.

"It's insane. Did you see him? He was the one that told me to stay earlier," Dorian continued.

"The blond one. Looked like a fallen angel. Yeah, I remember him."

"He said his name was Quinn, and he pushed this into my hand. I don't know what to do with it. I couldn't accept something like this from someone I do know," Dorian said as he studied the gift. "It's got to be worth thousands."

"Tens of thousands," I corrected. "For a flawless ruby like that, and I can't even imagine how many carats worth of diamonds. But you should wear it."

"What?" Dorian seemed shocked.

"It's practically pulsing with protection magic. Royal blood magic," I continued. "Those are royal jewels, and it's alive with undead magic."

"That would almost be funny," Dorian said with a smirk.

"You should wear it," I said again. "At least until they leave. I'd feel better. I won't have to worry about you."

"It's that strong?"

"It is."

"All right then," Dorian said as he put the necklace on and then tucked the giant gem into his shirt. "It's warm, and I can almost feel a heartbeat."

"It's the vampire's," I said. "His last heartbeats before he died. They weren't all born vampires."

"Whoa," Dorian said.

"Yeah," I responded. "I need a coffee."

We walked up to the counter, and Viv had drinks ready for us. A few customers came through the door, and then I remembered the receipt.

I didn't think it was a real clue, but I only had three days. So I would leave no stone unturned. "Viv, can I ask you something really quick?"

"Anything."

"It's probably nothing, but the victim was in here yesterday morning before he died. I was hoping you might recognize him. And maybe you could tell us if you saw anything that might help."

"Is that why they came here?" Viv's eyes widened with panic, and her hand came up to her throat. "Do they think I had something to do with it?"

"I don't think they know he was here," I said. "It was a coincidence."

"First of all, you don't believe in coincidences," Viv gently scolded. "So don't try to sell me on that crap. Second of all, I'm sure they know a lot more than they're letting on."

"Either way, you're not in danger. If they thought you had something to do with it, then they would have…"

"Done something about it while they were here," Viv finished for me.

"Yeah. I think they truly just liked your shop."

"I've heard the victim's name was Torin Rathmore, but that doesn't ring a bell," Viv said.

"I've got pictures on my phone, but he's dead…"

"I've got it here," Dorian said and showed Viv a thumbnail of one of Torin's YouTube videos.

"Oh, him," Viv said with a sigh. "Oh, that's too bad. He was a nice young man… oh, so he was a vampire?"

"Yes."

"He didn't go by the name Torin," Viv said before clearing her throat. "He always told me his name was Terry."

"I guess he didn't want people to know who he was," I said. "Maybe he was afraid someone would hear his name and connect him with his channel."

"That makes sense. Sometimes you just want to get a cup of coffee and not be bothered," Viv said. "Oh, but you know what?"

"What?"

"I thought he worked at the library. I mean, I'd have had no idea that he was a YouTuber, right? He was always talking about going to work at the library, and he was just such a nice, quiet young man."

"I don't think he worked at the library, but if he was really going over there every day, there must have been a reason," I said. "Thanks, Viv."

Suddenly, I was glad I asked her about the receipt. If nothing else, I had a lead.

Chapter Ten

Dorian and I left the Brew Station and made our way over to the library. I noticed that several times, he reached up and felt the necklace under his shirt. It looked like he was checking to make sure it was still there.

"You okay?" I asked as we climbed the stone steps to the library entrance.

"I'm fine," he said dismissively. "But are you sure the only magic on this thing is protective?"

"Why do you ask?"

"I don't know. I feel weird."

"Weird how?" I asked and stopped in the middle of the steps.

"Like I said, I don't know. I guess I just feel like I really want to see him again," Dorian practically whispered.

That made me laugh, but then I instantly felt bad. "Dorian, there's no love magic on that pendant, if that's what you're asking. I wouldn't have let you put it on if there was."

"But you said yourself that the protection was blood magic. What if this is... I don't know... outside of your realm of expertise," Dorian said and then winced. "I'm sorry. I promise I'm not insulting your magical capabilities."

I chuckled again. "No offense taken, but I promise you there's no love spell on that necklace. I might not be able to do vampire blood magic any more than I can do Fae magic, but I can feel them."

"Yeah, there's no spell on there," Meri added from between our feet. "You just like that dude."

"Meri!" Dorian actually blushed.

"I'm going to agree with the cat."

"You two are the worst," Dorian protested.

"Why?" I asked. "It's okay. He seems to fancy you too, Dorian. He gave you a pendant worth a bazillion dollars dripping in protection magic. Plus, he was gorgeous. You didn't think so?"

"I'm not saying that." Dorian's blush went from pink to deep scarlet. "But he's a vampire."

"So?" At that point I'd all but forgotten that I was supposed to be going into the library to investigate a murder.

Dorian would always be one of my top priorities, and he'd been single for such a long time. Which wouldn't be a big deal if was what he wanted, but I knew it wasn't. I also knew that after his investigations of the Satanic Church, he was wary of non-born vampires.

It was understandable, but not all of them had become vampires through demonic means. Some of them were simply turned. And the one that was interested in Dorian was basically a prince.

"They threatened you," Dorian responded. "They're going to... I don't know... wreak havoc in Coventry if we don't do their bidding."

"I'm pretty sure that's mostly on Lothaire," I said, and I knew I might be reaching, but I'd seen the way Quinn had looked at Dorian. I'd heard the tone of his voice when he demanded Dorian stay back in the field.

And I'd seen the way Dorian looked at him too. There was no love magic in that necklace, but it was connected to Quinn's heart. And Dorian's was responding. That wasn't love magic, but it was... the magic of love.

Something had snapped into place in the Universe when the two of them met, and I was determined not to let Dorian miss out on it. Especially not out of fear.

"Yeah, but Quinn isn't doing anything to stop him," Dorian protested. "That's points off in my book."

"There's nothing to stop yet," I retorted. "Lothaire gave us three days. Perhaps Quinn has full faith in my ability to bring the guilty witch to justice."

"Perhaps."

"Or maybe he's biding his time until he really needs to step in," I offered.

"Perhaps."

"So, what I'm saying is, keep an open mind."

"Is this because you let a hot vampire slip through your fingers once?" Dorian teased, but as soon as he said it, I could tell he regretted it. "I'm sorry, that was in bad taste."

"It's fine," I said with a chuckle. "And no, that's not why. I love Thorn, and I made the right choice."

"I know, and that's why I'm so hesitant. I want to make the right decision too. The divorce with Isaac..."

"I understand, but I don't think you should judge all vampires based on Azriel and his biker gang."

"I don't think these royal vampires have made much better of an impression," Dorian answered.

"Give him a chance. That's all I'm saying. If you want to, that is."

"I'll think about it," Dorian replied with a wink.

With that, we went inside the library. It looked exactly the same as when my Auntie Amelda ran it, but it wasn't the same without her.

As we stepped onto the polished marble floor, the regular half of the library for the human patrons was to the left. To the right was the witch library. It was warded to keep the humans from even noticing it, so when they came into the library, they didn't even look that way.

Of course, that meant the head librarian had to be a witch, and while that job at one time belonged to Auntie Amelda, Pepper Skeenbauer-Crowe was the new witch in charge of the stacks.

As soon as we walked into the library, Pepper must have felt our presence, because she drifted into the lobby. The look on her face told me she was about to ask if she could help us, but recognition washed over her features. With that, she gave me a curt nod and headed off into the witch stacks.

"You guys are close, huh?" Dorian joked.

"Her husband doesn't like the family," I said as we trailed behind Pepper.

"What's not to like about you guys?"

"We're just not everyone's cup of tea," I shrugged.

"So, she comes from a giant, powerful magic family, and she married a dude that doesn't like them? Seems legit."

"And she ended up with the job running the library too," I said but then held a finger up to my lips.

I could hear Pepper a few stacks over, and she sounded as if she was frantically shuffling something. I was immediately suspicious given her icy greeting.

I motioned for Dorian to follow me and quickly walked toward the shuffling. Right as I rounded the corner, I saw Pepper slam a book closed and shove it back on the shelf.

"Do you guys need any help with anything?" Pepper finally asked in a voice an octave higher than her normal.

"No, we're doing fine. Just looking for a spell," I said.

"For the festival?" Pepper asked politely.

"Yes. Just looking for something to liven up a presentation," I lied. It seemed that Pepper didn't know about the vampire situation.

Although I didn't know how, I suspected it was because she'd refused to close the library for the festival. Or let someone else run things for a few days. She was… dedicated.

"I can help you," Pepper offered. "I have a few minutes before a meeting."

Suddenly, I got the feeling that she didn't want to leave us alone. But I'd lied about needing a spell, and I really wanted to take a look in that book.

On cue, Pepper's eyes flicked over to it. "What did you have in mind?"

"Oh, don't worry about us. We're going to head over to the water spell section. I know what I'm looking for," I said, and I watched Pepper visibly relax.

"Okay, well, I'll be over on the other side if you need me. I'm preparing a budget proposal to buy some local art to decorate parts of the library."

"That's a wonderful idea. Amelda would be so proud," I said. "We'll come find you if we need anything."

Pepper nodded again and then drifted away. It was kind of eerie the way she walked. With her long skirts dusting the floor, it really did look like she was almost floating. If I hadn't known for sure she was alive, I would have pegged her as a ghost. Especially with her nearly white platinum hair worn in a Gibson Girl updo and large, round wire-framed glasses. She was only in her twenties, but she dressed like someone from a long-gone era.

"What's in that book?" Dorian asked as soon as Pepper was gone.

"You read my mind."

We'd moved away from the shelf where she'd stowed the book to put Pepper at ease, but as soon as she was gone, I marched right back over to it. While I hadn't gotten a great look at the tome while it was in her hand, in her haste, Pepper hadn't shoved it all the way back in the shelf. So it was easy to find, and I plucked it from between the other books.

Instantly, I knew something was strange about the book. It was too light despite being a leather-bound edition of an old book on finding magical geodes.

When I cracked the cover open, I was both shocked and completely unsurprised at the same time. Half of the inside of the book had been carved out to make a small compartment, and inside of that was a key.

A key that Pepper had on her person when we came into the library and that she wanted to hide as soon as she saw us. But why?

I pulled the key out and held it up for Dorian. Since it was on a bronze ball chain, I slipped it over my neck, and then tucked the key into my shirt.

"What do you think it's for?" Dorian asked as I smoothed my shirt over the pilfered key.

"I don't know but given everything that's gone on in the last couple of days, I'd say it's entirely possible that it's relevant to the murder," I answered.

"How do we find out what the key opens?"

"We could always ask," I answered with a shrug.

"Do you really think that's going to work?"

"Probably not, but maybe... I mean, she obviously wanted to hide the key from me. If she knows I know about it, then maybe she'll just come out with it. If not, I can use my position in the coven to persuade her."

"You did banish the last round of witches who crossed you," Dorian said.

"It wasn't quite like that."

"Enhanced interrogation techniques," Meri said from between my feet.

He held up a paw and flexed his claws before starting to purr so loud it was almost disturbing. At some point, he'd snuck into the library behind us. Not that anyone would tell him to leave...

"We're not torturing her," I said. "Nor are we going to banish her... because of course, she's going to tell us what we need to know."

Dorian and Meri both looked at me skeptically.

"Well, follow me then, Debbie Doubters. I'll show you."

I left the magic section and began the walk across the grand lobby to the mundane side of the library. Dorian was half a step behind me, and Meri darted out ahead.

Because I was watching him to make sure he didn't suddenly stop and trip me, I didn't see the shadow to my left. At first it just looked like a blur caused by the sun glaring in through the glass doors, but it wasn't.

It felt like a cold steel trap closed around my throat. The icy metal spun me around just in time to see Dorian go flying across the library and slam, thankfully, into a heavy tapestry. If he'd hit the wall full-on, he might not have lived long enough for me to save him.

That was if I could get my neck out of the bear trap around it. But I was panicking, wasn't I?

My eyes focused on what had me snared, and I saw pale skin and glowing blue eyes. It was a vampire. Not Lothaire or Quinn. Another of the royal conclave who had stayed quiet.

Until that moment.

"Now is your end, witch," he hissed.

But his mocking tone was met with a much more familiar hissing. I couldn't move my neck or head, but I could still move my eyes. When I looked down, Meri had begun to claw savagely at the vampire's legs.

"Idiot cat!" he howled and kicked Meri away.

His black fuzzy body hit the wall so hard that it cracked the marble, but what that vampire didn't know was that Meri was cursed to live until both the Skeenbauer and Tuttlesmith witches died off. And that wasn't going to happen anytime soon.

I tried to speak as Meri got up and shook the marble dust out of his luxurious black fur. But the vampire's fingers tightened and threatened to crush my windpipe.

But I didn't need to speak to use magic. Still, it was hard to focus my intention when the edges of my vision began to blacken. I had to do something fast, otherwise, I would pass out. While I believed Meri could save me, I didn't want to put that theory to the test. Who knew how many people the vampire could hurt before the cat stopped him?

"Meri," was all I managed to choke out before the vampire's grip threatened to break my spine. I could feel my toes going numb, and despite everything I had fought against in the past, I was terrified.

Meri let out what I could only describe as a battle cry and charged for the vampire again. The vamp tried to kick him, but Meri saw it coming before he got the boot. He dodged and leapt up and... I was pretty sure he bit the vampire on the butt.

It was the vamp's turn to howl, and his grip loosened just enough for me to suck in three quarters of a breath. It wasn't much, but it was enough to keep me from passing out.

But as I tried to focus my magical energy on the vamp's stupid face, I wanted to hurt him bad, a blinding white light shot across the lobby from behind me. The light didn't hurt me. Instead, it actually made my abused windpipe feel better, but when it hit the vampire, he screamed and dropped to the floor.

I whirled around, and Pepper stood there. She'd discharged so much magic, I could swear her hair was steaming.

She wobbled a little as she stepped toward me but took a deep breath and steadied herself. "Help me drag him into the witch stacks," she said breathlessly. "There are only a couple of people in the regular section of the library, but I'm sure they heard that."

I nodded, and each of us grabbed the vampire under an arm. Pepper was spent, and I was still reeling, but we managed to drag him into the magic section.

While we were doing that, Meri was running back and forth rubbing against Dorian's legs. He managed to revive him, and Dorian limped into the magic stacks just as a couple of curious library patrons appeared on the other side of the lobby.

"Just some drunk festivalgoer who stumbled into the wrong building," Pepper said to the patrons with a wave.

Because of the veil, and because it was a decent cover story, they just chuckled and headed back to their books or research. As soon as they were gone, Pepper collapsed onto the floor. Not fully passed out, but she sat with her legs crisscrossed, her elbows on her knees, and her hands supporting her head.

"Do you have any food?" I asked.

Pepper let out a long sigh before sitting up straight and offering me her hands. "Please help me up. I don't think I can do it on my own."

Dorian took one of her arms and I took the other.

"I can handle this," I said to Dorian. "And then I can get you fixed up."

"I'm right as rain, Kinsley. Meri did a bang-up job. Thanks, cat."

Meri just harrumphed as Dorian and I pulled Pepper up. I knew there was a lot of bacon and salmon in his near future, though.

The magical side of the library had its own break room. We helped Pepper get in there and sat her down at the mahogany table. The magical break room was far more opulent than the one on the other side for Pepper's few mundane employees. They got an old kitchen table with mismatched chairs, a microwave, and a refrigerator that only ran on the bits of magic Pepper fed it to keep from buying a new one.

"This is nice," Dorian said as he slid into the chair across from Pepper.

"Let me get you guys a drink," I said and went to the giant stainless-steel fridge along the right-hand wall.

"It should have whatever you want," Pepper said. "As long as it's not booze. I had to put a limit on it."

"Witches sneaking in here to get free drinks?" I asked with a cocked eyebrow.

"Yeah, the ones who either didn't have enough magic to make it on their own or were just too lazy," she said. "They stopped coming into the library when the fridge would only give them Diet Coke. I had to break up at least a few parties before I warded the fridge."

I opened the refrigerator door, and on the eye level shelf were two Cokes, one Dr. Pepper, three sandwiches, and a plate of precooked bacon. I took the plate out and set it on the floor. Meri immediately padded across the room and dug in.

While he was munching on his post-saving-our-butts-again snack, I carried the drinks and sandwiches over to the table. I knew the Dr. Pepper must be for Pepper, so I set the bottle in front of her. She opened it and gulped down half before I was able to give one of the Cokes to Dorian.

Once the drinks were squared away, I sorted out the sandwiches. After everyone had a chance to eat and get their strength back, it was time to get down to business.

Chapter Eleven

"More bacon," Meri said as I threw the sandwich wrappers away.

He could have as much as he wanted, so I opened the fridge again. Inside, there was another mountain of bacon and a plate of salmon.

"There's salmon too," I said as I reached for the bacon.

"I'll take it," he responded before licking his chops. "I could get use to this."

He made it sound like the rest of his life he was neglected. But he'd just saved me and Dorian. Sure, Pepper helped considerably, but I might have been a goner before she got there if not for Meri.

I put the plates on the floor and went to the breakroom doorway. The vampire was hogtied with magical rope out in the stacks, but we could see him from inside the room. I just wanted to make sure he was still out cold before I began questioning Pepper, and he was.

So, I made my way back to the table, scraped a chair across the floor so I could sit really close to her, and sat down. Pepper looked alarmed but also resigned. She knew.

"You found the key," she said before I could even ask. "I'm so stupid sometimes. I genuinely thought you guys might just leave."

"Don't call yourself stupid," I chastised. "You made a mistake. People make mistakes. But you're going to make up for it by telling me exactly what's going on."

"I can't," Pepper said in a low, reluctant voice.

"I think you're misinterpreting the situation," I said. "You saved me, and while I appreciate that immensely, I want answers. I want to know what this key is," I said and pulled it out from my shirt, "and where it goes. Oh, and while you're at it, why don't you tell me why you were so determined to hide it from me?"

Pepper looked over at Dorian, but he wasn't going to help her. As the reality of her situation settled on Pepper's face, she slumped a little in her chair.

"Someone has been stealing books from the magical side of the library."

"What? Who? And did you tell Amelda? Did you tell anyone?"

While it was possible that something like that wouldn't have made it back to me, I doubted it. Not the way rumors traveled in Coventry. So I already knew the answer. If Pepper had told anyone about the book thief, I would have already known and dealt with it.

"I don't know who it is," Pepper said. "But the key... Okay, so I followed them one day. I was never able to get close enough to see their face, but they went to this house. And when they left the house, I found that key under a flowerpot. I tried to go in and get the books back, but the key wasn't to the front door. It wasn't even to the side door. There are metal doors that probably lead to a basement around the back of the house, but I couldn't go down there. Even being in the yard, I started to feel like someone was watching me. I might have been paranoid, but I thought it might be some sort of trap. So I left, but I took the key."

"And you didn't tell anybody?" I repeated.

"I was afraid I might get fired. For letting someone steal books and for being too big of a coward to go into that house."

"I don't think you're a coward for not going into the house. That was probably smart, although, you're more powerful than you give yourself

166

credit for, Pepper. What you did to stop that vampire… that was intense magic."

While I paused, Dorian cut into the conversation. "But you're not telling us why you needed to hide that key when we got here," Dorian said. "Why was it so urgent?"

"Because I didn't want you to think I was a killer," Pepper blurted out.

"Why would we think that?" Suddenly, I was intrigued.

"Because I said I never saw the thief's face," she admitted.

I chewed on that for a moment. "Wait, you said you didn't see their face. How do you know it was a man?"

She sighed. "That's why I was worried. I didn't ever get a good look at their… at his face. But I'm pretty sure it was a man. Not just because of his height and build, but because when I followed him to the house, he was wearing this red sweatshirt."

"So?" I asked. "What does that mean?"

"It was a limited-edition merch shirt. One that Torin Rathmore raffled off the chance to purchase in one of his videos. There were only a hundred of them, and they were expensive."

"And nobody else in town had one," Dorian put it together before I could.

"But he had one," I said.

"Yeah," Pepper breathed out. "I would assume he did."

"But that doesn't make any sense," I protested. "If it was Torin stealing the books, how did he get in here to take them? Only witches can come into this half of the library."

"Probably the same way he did," Pepper nodded at Dorian. "He had tens of thousands of super fans. Probably hundreds of thousands. Torin's channel had millions of subscribers. You don't think any of them were witches? Or that any of them might have sent him a sigil? If he asked for it, I'm sure he found at least one person willing to betray their coven to give him what he wanted."

"Okay," I said and took a deep breath. "So, we have a vampire murder victim stealing books from the witch stacks in the magical library. And then we have his royal family showing up to demand we get him justice immediately. But we also have one of those vampires attacking when we're getting close to a possible clue."

"It could be a coincidence," Dorian said gently. "I know you don't believe in them, but maybe the attack and our visit here were just bad timing."

"I don't think I can just assume that, though. I have to investigate the connection until I establish that it's not a connection."

"Good point," Dorian answered.

"So, what do we do with him?" Pepper asked and pointed at the vampire. "And what are you going to do with me?"

"Dorian, can you call Quinn and ask him to deal with his brother vampire?"

"You're assuming I have his number?"

"I can call Lothaire instead if you don't, but I feel like that will make things more complicated. Quinn seems to be on our side."

"Fine. Yeah. His number appeared in my phone after he gave me the necklace. I'll call him."

Dorian stood up and left the room. He obviously didn't want me to hear his conversation with Quinn, and if it were not for the whole murder investigation thing, I would have been super curious about that.

"What are you going to do about me?" Pepper repeated when Dorian was gone.

"I'm not going to do anything about you as long as it doesn't turn out you're involved."

"You still think I could be?"

"I'm leaving the matter open for now," I said and then added, "but I don't think you should worry."

Dorian stepped back into the room. "Quinn said that Lothaire and a couple of the other vampires are on their way. They want to speak to you."

"Well, then I think that's our cue to leave," I said and stood up.

"You're just going to leave me here with him?" Pepper asked, but she didn't sound afraid.

"It's how you're going to make it up to me. Just tell Lothaire what that vampire did, and that I'll speak to him soon. I'm sure it won't take long for them to get here. They move very fast."

I started for the door. Pepper looked like she was going to protest, but instead, she just closed the breakroom door after Dorian and I exited.

Once we were close to the library exit, I leaned down and whispered to Meri, "Stay here and listen in. I want to know if she says anything to that vamp. Keep yourself hidden in the stacks. Oh, and I want to know what she says to Lothaire."

Meri gave me a wink and slinked off to hide in the magic stacks before Pepper could open the breakroom door again and see him. Dorian and I left the library and hurried off to the car.

"You got the address, right?" Dorian asked as I started the car.

I sat there frozen for a second. The thought had never even crossed my mind.

But I saw a black Rolls Royce turn onto the street a few blocks down, and I knew we had to move. I pulled the car out of our parking spot and took off in the opposite direction.

"You don't have the address, do you?" Dorian asked a minute later when I still hadn't said anything.

"It's fine," I said and pulled the car over to the curb. "There's a map in the glove compartment. Take it out, please, and unfold it."

"You have a map?"

"It's old, but you just never know, right?"

"You have an old map of the town where you live in your car?" Dorian pressed.

I shrugged. "It was a gift from my dad. He was the town's archivist, remember? I guess I mostly keep it for luck, and to make sure I can always find my way home."

"That's actually pretty great," Dorian admitted.

"And now it's going to come in handy," I said as I removed the key from around my neck.

"I saw this on an episode of *Charmed*," Dorian said as he smoothed the map across his legs as best he could.

"I'm sure you've seen me do it before too, and no, I didn't get it from a TV show."

"Don't you need, like, candles and stuff?"

"We're in a hurry. I can make do."

"If it was anyone else, I'd be worried," Dorian said with a nervous chuckle.

"It's just a locator spell. We're not even looking for a person. Just the lock that fits this key. Easy-peasy, lemon squeezy," I said and then put the key back on.

"Hey, don't you need to hold it over the map and let it circle until it hones in on a location?"

"Like I said, we're in a hurry."

"But what about the spell?"

"The lemon squeezy thing was the spell. You watch too much television. Look at the map."

Dorian looked down and saw the glowing yellow light on one of the houses on the map. "Oh, wow."

"We've been friends for almost a decade, Dorian. You'd think you'd have a better idea of how this works," I said with a wink.

"How can I when it always seems to change?" he asked and looked at the map again.

"Exactly," I said and pulled the car away from the curb. "Anyway, you can put the map away. I've got the address."

***

The house was just as creepy as I expected. Not in a huge, haunted old mansion way, though. Nope, it was a small, white house with dilapidated siding and a roof that looked like half the shingles were ripped off after decades of neglect. The yard was nothing but overgrown weeds, and while the house wasn't in the best part of Coventry, it was a blight on the street.

I sighed deeply as the house's negative energy got to me. I wondered how long it had been since a happy family had lived there. I could feel years of tension, financial strife, alcoholism, and dysfunction off-gassing from the sad little house.

"You okay?" Dorian asked.

"This was a good place to hide something. I doubt anyone would ever willingly step foot in this place."

"It does feel a bit... hinky, doesn't it?" Dorian turned back to study the house again.

"That's a good way to describe it," I answered.

"So, what is it? Angry ghosts? A demon? Should we even go in there? Should I go in there? You know that, thanks to my history, I'm more susceptible to possession..."

"I think the only thing haunting that house is years of misery. It's like a stain. As long as we're not in there too long, we'll be fine."

"And if we are?"

"We'll just need a little sage to clear the stain," I said and started for the house.

"I feel like you're downplaying this."

"Since when are you scared to investigate?" I asked, but I stopped. Maybe he was picking up on something I'd missed.

"I'm not. I don't know... it just feels... icky. Like something dark and sticky trying to..."

"Stick to us. Yeah, but don't worry. We don't have to go into the house. Just the basement that's locked from the outside."

"You really know how to wind a dude over," Dorian said, but he followed me through the yard.

The back yard was surrounded by an old chain-link fence, but it wasn't locked. The sidewalk around the side of the house and out to the back was more cracked and crumbled than it was not, but it was still better than walking through the weeds. I imagined those were full of snakes, rats, and poison ivy.

We got around to the double metal cellar doors that led to the basement. I'd halfway expected them to be padlocked, but the key was for a lock below the right metal handle.

I unlocked the doors, flung them both open, and then tentatively made my way down the concrete stairs to another set of doors. We lucked out that the exterior basement steps were in better shape than the sidewalk, and the interior set of doors were unlocked.

Through the doors, I ran face-first into a small chain. I knew from experience that it was most likely a light, so I tugged it gently.

Sallow, yellow light flooded the space around me. The room was long and rectangular with a dirty concrete floor. The other side had worn linoleum covering the concrete, and there was an old washer and dryer next to a utility sink. To my left was a hole halfway up the wall that probably went to a dirt crawlspace.

"There are no books," Dorian observed.

I looked around the dingy space again, and realized he was right. The only things down there besides the washer and dryer were three metal shelves and a mop bucket. I crossed the room to the rusty shelves to take a closer look.

While there weren't any books on the shelves, there were a couple of water-damaged cardboard boxes.

When I opened the first box, a big black spider darted out. His name was Fred, and he didn't scare me, but Dorian jumped up high enough that he nearly cracked his head on the low ceiling.

"How were you ever an investigative reporter?" I asked as I looked through the box. It contained nothing but two old Christmas mugs and a mostly empty bottle of dish soap.

"I just don't like it here," Dorian said as I opened the next box.

"No spiders in this one," I announced, "but look at this."

I pulled out an old leather-bound journal and held it up for Dorian. He took it and said "Awesome, let's go."

"Wait a second."

"Why?"

"Because look at these, Dorian."

Next to the box was a half-empty pack of "organic" cigarettes. The green and gold label, that seemed anything but organic in my opinion, sparked a memory.

I pulled out my phone and tabbed to the picture I'd taken of the deceased. Sure enough, a pack of the same kind of cigarettes stuck out of his jacket pocket.

A dull thud on the ceiling above us had me agreeing that it was time to go. I slid my phone back into my purse along with the pack of smokes and the journal.

"Please tell me we're not going to investigate who that is?" Dorian inquired as we headed for the cellar doors.

"It could be the killer."

"Kinsley."

I wanted to protest, but he was spooked. I'd never seen Dorian looked so rattled.

"Fine," I said and thrust my purse into his hands. "Go back to the car. I'll go look."

"Oh, no. You don't get to be the brave one while I get sent to the car like a scaredy pants crybaby," Dorian thrust my purse back at me.

"That's the spirit," I said. "Maybe we can end this whole thing right now."

"Or maybe it will end us," Dorian said.

But I ignored him and headed for stairs leading up to the inside of the house.

Chapter Twelve

"You almost peed your pants over a raccoon," I said with a chuckle.

"This place sucks, and it is very unkind of you to make fun of me for..." Dorian started to say.

But I cut him off. "I know. I'm sorry. I was a little freaked out too, but I was really hoping we could just bust a killer and get back to partying at the festival."

"When is it ever that easy?" Dorian shrugged.

"At least we have a clue now," I said.

"What's that, the journal? How do you even know it's connected to the case?"

"That I don't know. I haven't had a chance to read it yet, and it doesn't have any names on it that jump out at me. But the clue is the cigarettes. Remember, they're the same as the ones in Torin's pocket."

"Right, sorry. I must have had an adrenaline-induced amnesia. And also my rational mind tells me that it's probably just a coincidence. Not many people smoke anymore, but if that company is still making that brand, then it means more than one person smokes them."

"It could still be a clue, and one that might not be too hard to follow up on. There's only one little shop in town that sells this brand."

"How do you know that? You aren't a secret smoker, are you?" Dorian narrowed his eyes.

"No, but Lilith is," I said.

"Of course it's Lilith."

That made me chuckle. In my family, if someone was doing something they shouldn't, it was probably Auntie Lilith.

"I'd say something, but it's not like they can actually hurt her. She's got a tattoo on her arm that's some sort of sigil protecting her from the effects of smoking."

"Really? That's kind of cool. We don't even have a tattoo shop here in Coventry."

"She got it from a friend when she was on one of her adventures," I said with a shrug. "It was a long time ago."

"And besides, the smokes are organic. I'm sure it's basically the same as eating vegetables."

I rolled my eyes. "Don't get me started on that."

"I won't because I want to get out of here. Even if it was just a raccoon, this place is still giving me the heebie-jeebies. Let's go to that smoke shop and see what they have to say."

We left the house the way we came in through the basement since I didn't have a way to lock the front door deadbolt behind us. As soon as we were back downstairs, the raccoon started thumping around again. Probably brought his whole family for his little raccoon party.

The smoke shop that sold the organic cigarettes was over in what I like to affectionately think of as the 'tavern district.' Most small towns had a competition between taverns and churches. As far as which one there was the most of... In Coventry, taverns won because so many residents were witches. We just didn't have as many churches.

But nestled in between two of the dive bars was a little smoke shop. It looked like something out of a bygone era. Mostly because it was. Smoking had largely been eradicated, but since supernaturals could still smoke, and there were some diehard humans who wouldn't give the habit up too, some cigarette companies managed to stay in business.

And in little towns like Coventry, you could still find old-fashioned smoke shops. Dried tobacco smelled amazing when it wasn't burning, and that rich, complex scent hit us when we walked through the door.

The shop was small in that the building that housed it was very tall but narrow. There were several rows of shelves placed quite close together, and in the center of the shop was a tight aisle that lead to a counter in the back.

Since we weren't there to shop, both Dorian and I made our way single file to the counter in the back. Behind the counter was a short, stout man thumbing through a hunting magazine and smoking a pipe.

He kept reading for a few seconds before dramatically closing the magazine and looking up at us. "Help you?"

"Actually, you can," I said as cheerfully as possible given his complete lack of customer service skills. I pulled the cigarettes out of my purse and placed them on the counter.

"I don't have any," he said and opened his magazine.

"You don't sell them here?"

"Didn't say that. Said I don't have any. Sold out and my next shipment won't be here for two days. Better make 'em last, or you'll need to smoke a different brand."

"These aren't mine," I said, and the man cocked an eyebrow at me.

"Then what are you in here bugging me for? Can't you see I'm trying to read my magazine?"

"I was hoping you could tell me more about this man," I said and looked at Dorian.

"What about him?" he asked before taking a puff of his pipe.

"No, I mean... Dorian, could you show him a picture? Like one where Torin's alive, please?"

"On it." Dorian pulled out his phone and thankfully, he'd already taken the time to find a picture of Torin alive, because I felt like we'd already lost the tobacco shop man's attention.

Dorian showed the phone to the man, and he responded with, "What about him?"

"He's dead. You might have picked up on that."

"And?"

"Well, he smokes those cigarettes. You're the only shop in town that sells them. As far as I know…"

"I am, but that dude does not buy them here."

"He doesn't?" I asked.

"Nope. Really only one chick who does. I keep a carton on hand for her, but she bought the last two packs a couple of days ago. Supply chain disruptions and such, so I don't have them in stock again."

"You said only one woman buys them?"

"That's what I said. Just this one chick."

"Can you tell me who she is?" I asked hopefully.

"Why?"

I took a deep breath and tried not to sigh. "Because we found these cigarettes on a dead guy."

"That's gross, lady. Could you get them off my counter?" he said and then bent over and started rustling around underneath the counter. "See if I got some all-purpose down here. Wish I had some of that bleach stuff. Like for the bathroom…"

"Not this pack," I said. "The dead guy had a pack on him. I found this one... somewhere else."

"Oh," he said and sat back up, completely abandoning his quest to clean the counter. "I'm no snitch. You two law enforcement?"

"She's a witch. And I'm a gay werewolf," Dorian cut in.

"Dorian!" I scolded.

But the man chuckled. "You don't say?"

"I don't," I said.

That made him laugh again. "You two are all right. Chickie who buys that brand of smokes from me has the name of Odessa Brack. She works over at that ice cream place. The new one over in the strip mall. Scoops of Fun... Yeah, that's the one. Anyway, I bet she's a heaping scoop of fun."

"What do you mean?" I wished I had asked as soon as the words slipped out.

"Oh, just that she's a real looker. Bubbly and blonde. You'll know her when you see her for sure. But you might have to ask for her because she's the manager. So she's not always out front."

"You seem to know a lot about this woman?" Dorian asked, he managed to keep his tone pretty lighthearted.

The man studied him for a moment. "Well, I guess I do," he belted out a hearty laugh. "She comes in here to get her smokes every couple of days, and we get to talking. Nothing untoward, though. She's young enough to be my daughter. Pretty girls that young are too much trouble for an old guy like me. I keep things simple. I like my pipe and my magazines."

"Do you do any hunting?" I asked. We needed to get going, but I felt bad taking the information and running off.

"Nah. In fact, I'm practically a vegetarian. Just been reading this magazine since I was a kid. I like the pictures of the great outdoors."

"I'll have to take a look at one sometime," Dorian said before latching his arm around mine. "Welp, we gotta get going. Thanks for all your help."

Dorian spun me around and we started for the door. "Thanks so much," I said over my shoulder and offered the guy a wave with my free hand.

"Well, that was fun," Dorian said as we made for the car.

"I can't believe you told him I was a witch and you were a gay werewolf..."

"It worked, didn't it?"

"But how did you know it would? You realize something like that could backfire spectacularly."

We were back to the car and both got in before continuing the conversation. Dorian and I buckled our seatbelts, and he pulled away from the curb. I just assumed we were headed for Scoops of Fun.

"That guy seemed like a simple kind of guy, but he also came off as a little bored. So I entertained him a little. Make someone laugh, and they'll take to you. It forces a bond, but it feels good. So I don't feel bad about doing it."

"Hmm... I do have to wonder if you use that kind of manipulation on me," I pondered.

"Of course not," Dorian said and gave me a wink.

A couple of minutes later, we pulled into the strip mall parking lot. There weren't many cars out in front of Scoops of Fun, so we were able to get a close spot.

As soon as we walked inside, I knew the person scooping ice cream for the shop's three customers wasn't Odessa. It was an older woman, probably in her seventies, but she had a bright smile and strong arms.

We waited in line behind the other customers, but I perused the selections. Every flavor looked so tempting, and the weather outside was perfect for an ice cream cone. I knew I should probably bring the girls in there some time to get a treat, but why shouldn't I get a little something while I was there?

"What flavor are you getting?" Dorian asked.

"Rocky road sundae with marshmallow sauce and perhaps some hot fudge too. Okay, definitely some hot fudge too. Oh, and maybe some of those mini marshmallows and extra peanuts. What about you?"

Dorian just looked at me for a second. He blinked a few times. All the years that we had been friends, and my food shenanigans still managed to shock him sometimes.

"That actually sounds really decedent and tempting, but I think I'd ruin my dinner."

"I don't think I've ever ruined my dinner before, so sorry I can't relate. But I'm pretty sure that even if I could, I would. I mean, what are you even going to have for dinner? Was it something special?"

"You know, you're absolutely right," Dorian agreed.

When it was our turn, Dorian stepped up to the counter and put in the order for our sundaes. But before the woman could walk off to make them, I stopped her. "Hey, also, is Odessa working today? We'd really like to speak with her."

"Is there a problem?" the woman behind the counter asked.

"No. Not really. We just need to talk to her," I said.

The woman eyed me suspiciously, but ultimately acquiesced. "Give me just a second. I'll go get her before I start on those sundaes."

"Thank you."

Two minutes later, the woman reappeared from the back. "Odessa is on a call with one of our suppliers, but she'll be up here as soon as she can."

"Thank you," I replied.

"If you guys want to have a seat, I'll bring your ice cream out to you when I'm done."

"Thanks," Dorian answered.

The previous three customers had taken their ice cream and left. It was just Dorian and me in the shop, so we took the best table. To me, that was the one by the large front window. Sure, the view was just the parking lot, but you could still see the nice trees and flowers that made up the strip mall's professional landscaping.

Eventually, a woman emerged from the back of the ice cream shop behind the service counter. And the man at the tobacco shop had been right about her. She was statuesque and blonde with a smile that lit up the room.

Probably because she had her 'customer service' face on, but Odessa still seemed sweet and approachable as she came and sat down at our table.

"How can I help you folks today? Surely you didn't have any issues with Gladys, right?" she asked and turned to the woman behind the counter. Gladys gave her a wave, and Odessa winked. "She's my best. I'm sure she'll have those sundaes right up, and they will be the best you've ever had."

"I'm sure they will be," I said quickly. "I'm sorry to ambush you like this, Odessa, but we're not here to talk about the shop. I came to ask you about Torin."

Odessa's face turned dark and stormy in an instant. A single tear immediately escaped from each of her eyes, but her mascara held as she wiped them away with the back of her hand.

"Oh, dear," she said and breathed out heavily. "It's so terrible."

"We're not with the police," Dorian cut off her next question. It was always their next question. Well, almost always.

"But, I'm the person in charge of the Beltane Festival, and well..."

"Those vampires are breathing down your neck," Odessa leaned over and whispered.

"You know about that?" I stated.

"Yeah, and I knew about Torin too. It would be kind of hard to be in a relationship with someone like that and not know."

"That makes sense."

"But you're not?" Dorian posed the question, so I didn't have to.

"I am a daughter of Skadi. That's the Norse Goddess of snow and other wintry things. She's also a giantess. That's why I'm so tall. But I don't have any magical powers really. I just like being around cold things. Hence why I work here. Oh, and I can tell when others are magical," Odessa was still whispering all of this, and she clammed up as Gladys approached with our sundaes.

"Here you go," Gladys said as she put the sundaes on the table in front of us. "I hope everything is okay."

"Everything is great, Gladys. In fact, why don't you take your break while we're slow. I'll keep an eye on things up here."

"You sure, boss?"

"Absolutely."

While they talked, I dug into my sundae. It was delicious, and I had to force myself to slow down. First, so I didn't end up with brain freeze, and second, so I didn't look like a lunatic shoveling huge spoonfuls of ice cream into my mouth like it was my job.

After an additional thirty seconds or so of chitchat, Gladys walked away. Odessa turned her attention back to me. "So, what is it you want to know? I'm not sure I can tell you too much about Torin recently. We broke up a while ago, and I... haven't kept up with him."

"You don't have any idea who could have killed him?" I asked because I couldn't just come out and ask her if she did it.

"He had a lot of fans who were obsessed with him. Like, really obsessed. To the point it kind of scared me, but Torin just ate it up. He didn't seem to be afraid of anything, though. I guess that comes with the territory of being an immortal."

"Was that a problem for you?" Dorian asked. "Him having fans that were obsessed with him? Lots of other women interested in him?"

"And men too," Odessa added. "And yeah, I guess sometimes it did make me a little jealous. Especially when he ignored me to soak up all of that attention, but if you're asking me if I killed him? No. Like I said, we broke up a while back."

"Was that hard for you?"

"No, I didn't kill him because he dumped me," Odessa said flatly. "I know that's what you're thinking. But I broke it off with him. And yes, it was difficult, but it was absolutely the right thing to do."

"Why is that?" I asked as gently as I could.

"We weren't right for each other, but he did get weird after I broke things off," Odessa said without looking me in the eye.

"How so?"

"He didn't take it well."

"You realize that without giving me more details, that could make you sound even more like a suspect," I said.

"I wanted to move on with my life, and he seemed determined to keep that from happening. But it was more annoying that anything. He scared me sometimes, but it was more for him than me being afraid he'd do something to me. I'm convinced that if he wasn't a vampire, he'd have hurt himself."

"He was wearing a locket with a picture of himself in it when he died, Odessa," I said because I felt like the necklace had something to do with her, but she wasn't coming out and saying it. "It looked... very feminine given his aesthetic."

She sighed. "Yeah, he'd given that to me, and I gave it back when we broke up. It was an expensive necklace, and I didn't feel right keeping it. He told me to take the picture out of it and put another in, but I just didn't want it. He wore it every day after that. You can see it in any videos he made after we split."

"You kept watching his videos?" Dorian pressed.

"I didn't, but I know a lot of people who do. He is... he was very popular. They told me."

"Is there anything else you want to tell us?" I asked. "Because my husband is investigating this murder, but ultimately, I'm going to decide... what happens."

"I get why you're asking, but I didn't kill him," Odessa said flatly. "I was here that morning. Gladys can confirm it. So can the security cameras the owner installed to keep the teenage employees who work here after school from stealing ice cream."

"I see," I said. "Well, thanks for talking to us."

Odessa left our table after that and retreated to the back of the ice cream shop. Dorian and I finished our sundaes, and I was about to leave when Dorian stopped me.

"Aren't you going to check her alibi?"

"It seems pointless. Why would she lie if she knew we could check it without even leaving the shop?" I asked.

"Because she might have counted on you assuming that exact thing," Dorian said and waited for me to say something. When I just shrugged, he continued, "Fine, I'll go ask her."

"Dorian, it's fine. I'm sure we don't need to..."

But he was already up and headed for the counter. I wasn't sure how Gladys was going to react to strangers asking for an alibi for her boss, so I totally ditched Dorian and went out to wait by the car.

Less than five minutes later, he walked out the ice cream shop's door. "You were right," he said as we got into the car. "She confirmed her boss's alibi."

"I told you."

"Well, I wanted to know for sure. Now we know for sure."

"Thanks," I said. "You didn't have to do that."

"I just..."

Dorian was about to finish his statement and start the car, but an argument interrupted. Two raised voices, one male and one female, made us whip around.

Those shouts came from none other than two of my employees from Summoned Goods & Sundries. Sol and Azura stood next to his car a few feet spaces away from us. I hadn't noticed them pull into the lot, but it appeared that they'd planned on going to Scoops of Fun together. Unless they were there to get their nails done, get a tan, or see the dentist.

But they were not having scoops of fun. Not in the least.

Chapter Thirteen

"I want to go home right now," Azura snarled.

Sol ran both of his hands through his hair so hard it pulled his forehead back and raised his eyebrows. "Woman..."

"Don't call me woman!"

"Azura."

"Ugh, I hate it when you say my name too."

"Azura, tell me what to do here. You want me to take you home, fine."

"This was your idea," she groused.

"And ten minutes ago, you were more than happy to go along with it."

"Yeah, well, that was until you almost wrecked the car staring at Lucy Jizmajian."

"Lucy! This is about Lucy! Oh, come on, Azura. I wasn't staring at her. She stepped out in front of the car. I was trying NOT to kill us."

"I'm sure that little purple skirt she was wearing didn't help."

"You are impossible!"

"No, Sol. You are impossible. Impossible to read and impossible to deal with."

"I am not impossible to read. You're just bound and determined to hate me, Azura."

"I don't hate you," she said as all the fight left her.

"And I am not impossible to read."

"Are you guys okay?" Dorian asked, and both of their heads whipped around as Sol and Azura noticed us for the first time.

"Yeah, what's wrong, you guys?" I asked.

"Nothing," Sol said in frustration. I think that was the thing that startled me the most. Normally, Sol was so positive, but his little spat with Azura had definitely clouded over his usual sunshine. "Azura was hungry, so I offered to get her something to eat after work. This is where she wanted to go," he said and waved toward Scoops of Fun.

"Don't put this on me," she said as the petulance returned to her voice.

"I'm not putting anything on you, Azura. I thought this was what you wanted. When you said you wanted to get something to eat..." But then his face went a little slack, and I saw a lightbulb go off in his mind.

Of course, I was still confused. "I have no idea what is going on, but the two of you need to stop yelling at each other out in front of an ice cream shop."

"I'm sorry," he said to Azura, and she looked suddenly stricken. "I get it now what you meant when you said you sure would like to get something to eat."

"You do?"

"Will you go out to dinner with me?"

"What is even going on here?" Dorian interrupted.

"Shhhh," I said and backhanded his stomach.

"And no, I wasn't looking at Lucy. I was trying not to get in an accident with you in the car, because you are what matters. I'm not interested in her at all. I'm only interested in you, Azura. I have been since the day I met you. You're the only one I look at."

"What is actually going on here?" Dorian leaned over and whispered to me.

"He's asking her out," I whispered back. "Won't they make an adorable couple?"

"Mr. Sunshine and Mrs. Storm Clouds with a side of chip on her shoulder? Oh, they're just perfect."

"They complement each other," I insisted. "They balance each other out."

"Whatever you say. Can we get going?"

"I want to hear what she says."

Dorian shut up, and we turned our attention back to Sol and Azura. They were locked in an embrace, so I figured the answer must have been yes.

We took that as our cue to leave and went back to the car. After that, we went back to the festival. While I was doing what I had to do to keep everyone safe, I felt like I was neglecting my duties there.

Of course when we arrived, I found that everything was running just fine without me. "I think I'm going to go home for a while," I told Dorian a short time after we got there. "I need a break from everything."

"That's understandable," Dorian answered. "Do you want me to drive you?"

"No, stay and have fun if you want. You can always call me and let me know if you need me to come back. I think I might spend the night in my bed tonight if things are going okay here, though."

"Over it already?" Dorian asked, but there was no judgment in his voice.

"I thought it would be different. I mean, I knew it would be work, but I thought it would be more fun too. I just..."

"I totally understand. It probably would have been different if you hadn't had all of this murder and vampire stuff going on."

"You're right, but now I feel exhausted."

"Go home, then. I'm sure Thorn and the girls will be thrilled you did. I'm going to stay, though. I'll call you if you need to come back."

"Thanks, Dorian."

"You can thank me by letting me have the ridiculous tent of yours for the night. You know, since you won't be using it."

"Of course," I said with a chuckle. "Have a good time. Don't do anything I wouldn't do."

He winked at me and then headed off into the crowd. I wondered what he was up to, and for a split second, I could have sworn I saw a flash of luxurious blond hair in the crowd. A man in a red velvet suit with a smile too beautiful to really exist. But then they were both gone.

"Good for him," I said to myself as I headed back to my car.

I drove home with my mind split between the journal we found and a big pot of spaghetti. The pasta I'd make for dinner, and I hoped the journal contained some sort of clue.

Because I really had no idea what was going on. Love was in the air as the Beltane spirit surrounded us like a warm spring breeze, but I was up to my neck in death. Literally, since vamps were involved.

When I got home, no one was there. The girls were still with my parents, and Thorn was at work.

Meri must have been off doing Meri things. So I went inside and put the journal on the kitchen counter while I prepared to make dinner.

I sent my mom a text message letting her know I was home. *Please bring the girls home for dinner? I making spaghetti if you and Dad are interested.*

Everything okay? Mom texted back.

Just needed these familiar walls for the evening.

We'll see you for dinner, she replied.

And that was that. I still had some time before I needed to start cooking, so I grabbed a Coke from the fridge and sat down at the kitchen table with the journal.

I cracked it open and began to read. I realized very quickly that the journal wasn't old or particularly significant. It just looked like an old, leather tome with worn pages, but it was the kind of thing you could pick up on the internet for about twenty dollars.

The bulk of what it contained were notes and mini scripts for Torin's show. There were a few personal entries, but they were mostly about other YouTube celebrities. I paid close attention to those in case there was something significant enough to make it a clue.

A lot of it was catty, and some of it was downright childish, but none of it was worth killing over. At least not in my opinion. So it wasn't anything I would investigate unless I got a lot more desperate.

I flipped the pages and saw something that did pique my interest. Scrawled in the margins was a note. "Need the bone of a murderer for ritual."

What the flip did that mean? I mean, I knew that such body parts were used with black magic rituals, but why did Torin need it? Could he have somehow been involved in dark magical practices? But why? And where did he learn them?

Or was the journal even his? It had notes and scripts in it, but the scrawl was cursive and his other notes were in print. So I couldn't tell exactly if it was his writing or not.

I did the same thing, though. Since I'd learned both print and cursive in school, I sometimes alternated which I used depending on how fast I was trying to write.

Just as I set the book down on the kitchen table and started pondering, Meri wandered into the kitchen. "You look like you're in pain."

"I'm trying to think."

"Well, definitely don't hurt yourself, then," he snarked.

"You need new lines."

"Please, I'm hilarious."

"Dang it," I said as I lost my train of thought. Turning my attention to Meri, I asked, "What did you hear at the library?"

"Nothing."

"What do you mean, nothing? You were supposed to listen in when the vamps showed up to pick up the guy that attacked me."

"Yeah, they didn't say anything."

"They didn't say anything? At all?"

"Nope. They stood in the lobby and waited for that chick to drag him out too. It was kind of weird."

"They made Pepper drag him out into the lobby?"

"Yes," Meri confirmed.

"But they didn't tell her to do it?"

"No, they just stood there creepily staring at her until she did it. Well, I guess I helped."

"Drag him out?"

"Oh, nope. I mean... Thinking back, I could have done that. But anyway, I suggested maybe she should drag the vampire out."

"Oh," I said.

"And when she did, they took him and left."

"Meri, did you talk to Pepper after they left? Did she have any ideas about why they acted like that?"

"You never said anything about that. Do you have any bacon?"

I sighed. "Yeah, let me get some and cut it up," I said and got up from the table.

As I cut up his bacon, I thought about what the exchange, or lack thereof, between Pepper and the vampires meant. Most likely, it meant that she had nothing to do with any of this.

Or it meant they knew Meri was there. But that seemed almost impossible. If Meri wanted to be invisible, he was invisible.

"So what's with the book?"

"Right, before you came in and so rudely interrupted me..."

"Hey, I was delivering the information you asked for," Meri interrupted.

I sighed. "Anyway, I was combing through the book looking for clues. I think it was Torin's notebook. Not really a journal. But there's a note in the margin on the page I left open. It says something about needing the bone of a murderer for a ritual."

"That sounds like a clue."

"It would be, but I can't be certain that Torin wrote that part. Or any of it, actually."

"Why would someone else write a note about needing a bone in Torin's notebook?"

"That's what I was trying to work through when you showed up," I said.

"You could... I don't know... do a spell..." Meri groused.

"I was going to arrive at that very conclusion if you hadn't interrupted my thinking," I said and brought the plate of bacon to the table for him.

"And spared you pain. I saved you."

"I'm going to get some candles. If I'm going to do a spell to find out if the handwriting is from the same person, I need to get it done. I've got to make spaghetti."

"Ohhh. And meatballs?"

"Of course."

A few minutes later, I had the various candles, herbs, and salt I needed to do the spell on the book. I pushed the book into the center of the table and then lit the candles.

"That's awfully fancy considering you just want to know if the same person wrote the note," Meri said as he sashayed back over to the table. "It's good that you're taking magic more seriously, I guess."

"It's not that fancy," I protested.

"It is considering you're going to do the same thing no matter what you find out," Meri suggested.

"What? What do you mean?"

"What are you going to do if it was Torin who wrote the note?" Meri asked.

"Go to the cemetery and see if anyone has dug up a grave recently," I answered.

"What are you going to do if it wasn't him?"

"Same thing," I admitted.

"I'd say save your candles and such for when you have more information," Meri suggested. "Let's just go to the cemetery."

"I need to make spaghetti."

"And meatballs."

"Right, and the meatballs. Plus, at some point, I need to go check on the festival... I guess. It's probably fine if you're not there. It's just a bunch of witches partying. I'm sure they can manage that on their own."

"Meatballs."

"Yeah, and Dorian said he'd call me. I'm sure he'll call if anything goes sideways."

"Unless he gets sacrificed because the evil witch needs shifter blood too," Meri said completely deadpan.

"Oh, no."

"I'm kidding," Meri said with an eyeroll. "Calm down, Kinsley. He's not even really a shifter anymore."

"Right. Right. Okay."

"Besides, you wanted to spend the evening with your family."

"I did, but now I'm going to end up going to the cemetery to investigate."

"You're really no good at this."

"At what?" I asked.

"Anything."

"Whatever."

"Whatever," Meri groused.

"Anyway, I'm going to make the spaghetti."

"And the meatballs."

"You are obsessed."

"Make me four."

"Fine."

My parents came for dinner, and it was a pleasant meal. Mom and Dad offered to take the girls for the evening, and I almost took them up on it.

"I really should let you take them," I said to Mom. "I was going to stay home this evening, but I need to go to the cemetery and look into something."

"Oh, what's that?" she asked with an eyebrow raise.

"There's a clue in the journal about needing the bone of a killer for a ritual. I wanted to go to the cemetery and see if any graves have been disturbed recently. But I also just wanted to spend the evening with the girls and Thorn. I'm so torn."

"Because you felt guilty enough about your festival duties, and now you feel like you have to ditch both your family and the festival because of the murder," Mom said without judgment.

"But I have to because if I don't, these vampires are going to cause a lot of trouble."

"Mom," I heard just before someone tugged at the sleeve of my shirt.

It was Laney. She'd been sitting with her sister on the sofa, but at some point while my mother and I were talking, she'd crossed the room like a silent ninja.

"What is it, sweetie? Grandma and I were just saying our goodbyes."

"Promise you won't be mad?"

"Uh-oh," Mom said knowingly.

"Laney, how can I promise not to be mad when I don't know what you're about to tell me?"

"You have to swear."

"Okay. All right. I swear I won't be mad."

Mom whistled. But in truth, I never really got mad at the girls. Annoyed? Yes. And sometimes, I guess I did get angry, but I kept my emotions in check. Laney had never asked me to swear to not get angry. So whatever she had to tell me, it had to be a doozy.

"I have a history fair project due in two days, and I forgot about it."

"Oh."

"Well, that's not such a big deal," Mom interjected. "We can just…"

"We can't use any magic. The teacher wants us to learn how to complete tasks without using our powers, so each project will be tested for magic. Any hint of the supernatural, and it's an automatic fail."

"In two days?" I asked feeling my stomach drop. I'd read horror stories on the internet about history fair projects ripping families apart. It was worse than playing *Monopoly* at family game night. And that was when people had more than two days to complete the assignment. "How long have you known this was due? I can't believe the teacher gave you guys such a short deadline."

Laney's face blanched. "Three months ago. I just... I kept forgetting about it. I really meant to tell you."

I just stood there for a moment blinking. I'd open my mouth to say something and then close it again. Because I was angry. Real good and angry, and I didn't want to say anything I couldn't take back. Besides, she was eight. It was an eight-year-old mistake, and I needed to calm down.

"Laney," Mom said as I stood there blinking and blobbing like a fish out of water, "I think this is one of those times where you're going to have to learn about consequences. You cannot expect your mother to fix this. You're just going to have to take the bad grade."

"It's fifty percent of our history grade," Laney choked back tears. "I won't pass."

"Oh," Mom said.

"And then she won't go on to fourth grade," I added.

"That's too much of a consequence," Mom practically whispered.

"I agree," I said and resolved myself to helping Laney finish her hellish history fair project in two days.

"But the vampires," Hekate said from the sofa where she'd been happily enjoying her sister's torment.

"How do you know about that?" I asked and turned to my mom.

"Don't look at me. I didn't tell her anything."

"Everybody knows," Laney said with a sniffle. "I'm so sorry."

"We'll fix this," I said and put my arm around Laney. "But you're going to have to put in the work. I'll help you, but I'm not doing it for you."

"I can take a couple of vacation days," Thorn said as he appeared from the dining room.

"You can't," I answered. "We need you and your deputies keeping an eye on the town. You might not be witches, but we need you out there protecting Coventry."

I could have sworn his chest puffed out a little. But it was true. We needed him.

"The offer is on the table," Thorn said.

"Laney, why don't you get anything you have that tells us about the history project and start going over it with your Dad. I need to talk to Grandma, and then we'll put our heads together."

"Thanks, Mommy," she said and wrapped her little arms around my waist. I could feel the relief emanating off of her.

Thorn and Laney retreated into the dining room with her backpack and Bonkers in tow. "You should do your project on the history of donuts," Bonkers said as he followed right behind them.

"I'll go to the cemetery," Mom said as soon as they were gone.

"I can't ask you to get involved in this, Mom. It's my responsibility."

"I still believe the kids and Thorn are your first responsibility, and I know you feel that way too," she said. "But also, you're not asking me to do it. I'm volunteering. You're already trying to be in two places at once, which you literally cannot do, so please stop trying to be in three. I'll go to the cemetery with your father and check things out. I'll let you know what I find."

"Okay," I relented. "Thank you."

"You're welcome, sweetie. And you should stop thinking of this vampire mess as just your responsibility. It's my coven too. It's our coven. If I need to call the Aunties together, I will."

"I think we can handle it for now," I said. "Let's try ourselves for a little while longer. Some of the Aunties will want to go to all-out war with the vamps, and I want to avoid that if possible."

"Understood. Dad and I will go to the cemetery now. I'll report back if I find anything suspicious," Mom said.

"I'm going with them," Meri announced and darted out the door as soon as my dad opened it.

Chapter Fourteen

Brighton

Remy pulled the car down the cemetery road and parked it by a huge oak tree. The combination of the hill and the tree meant the car wouldn't be visible from the street. Not that I was too worried about Coventry law enforcement catching us in the cemetery after hours.

What were they going to do? Kinsley wouldn't feel right putting a sleep spell on a deputy and making her escape, but I had no problems with it.

"This good?" Remy asked.

"Yeah. So how do you want to work this? Should we stick together or split up? We could cover more ground split up."

"Isn't that how all horror movies start?" Remy asked.

"We can only hope," I said as I slid out of the passenger seat. "I could use a little excitement, if you know what I mean."

Remy laughed as he got out of the car. "I think we should stick together."

I shot him a look.

"Okay. Okay," he said and held his hands in front of his chest in mock surrender. "We'll split up. Is the cat going with you or me?"

"I'm out of here. Bye," Meri answered before darting off into the night.

"I guess I'm going too," Remy said. "I'll go that way and take that half, and you can take the half closest to the road."

"Is that so if we get busted, I have to deal with the cops?" I asked.

"I would never hide in the trees and let you take the heat, sweetie," Remy said with a wink.

"Yeah, yeah. Of course you wouldn't call me if you need anything," I replied. "Or you know, just holler."

"Will do, boss," he said with a mock salute and then started walking in the same general direction as Meri had taken.

That left me alone, in the moon light, to walk around the cemetery grounds. If I hadn't been looking for signs of grave robbery that also might be a clue to another murder, it would have been pleasant.

I liked to walk in the graveyard at night. In fact, if it had been any other week, I'd probably already know if something strange had gone on. It was so peaceful there, and I frequented it regularly.

Something about the sounds of crickets with an owl hooting made me feel alive. I looked around as the white light of the moon glimmered off the headstones. There was so much beauty even in mourning places.

But after a while, I'd walked every row and found nothing. I was closing in on the sections that were Remy's job to patrol, and I saw him off in the middle distance.

I waved, and he began walking toward me. But when he was about halfway, I realized it wasn't Remy at all.

It was Lilith. She had her long, gray curls tied up into a bun on the back of her head and wore a black T-shirt, worn jeans, and black combat boots. In one hand, she held a black drawstring bag and in the other, a small gardening spade.

"Lilith, what are you doing out here?" I asked once she was a few feet from me.

"Collecting graveyard dirt," she said and gave the bag a jostle. I could hear a couple of glass jars clang together. "What are you doing out here? Did you need graveyard dirt? Are you getting into necromancy?" She gave me a wide smile.

"No," I said.

"It's okay. Obviously, I think it's cool. Anyway, I've got some here, but if I don't have the right kind of grave for your... purposes, we can do the ritual to collect together."

"Lilith, I'm not here to get graveyard dirt for necromancy. I'm here looking for graves that might have been recently robbed. And you are out here with a shovel."

"A shovel? This is a tiny little gardening trowel," Lilith answered with a snicker. "It would take me hours to dig up an entire grave with this thing. I'm just here harvesting dirt. From the tops of the graves. I mean, sometimes I dig in a few inches just to get the most energetic dirt but..."

I interrupted here. "Did you see any graves that looked like they might have been dug up and reburied recently?"

"What kind of graves?"

"Why does that matter?"

Lilith let out an exasperated sigh. "You know, I would have raised you right."

"Anyway?" I asked and tapped my foot impatiently.

"I need to know what kind of grave because then we can look. Think about it, Brighton. I use this dirt all of the time for my shadow work. If it's a specific type of grave you're looking for, then I know where it is."

She was absolutely right.

"I think someone was looking for the bones of a killer. To grind up and use in a potion, perhaps."

"Ah, well, that does make things easier. There weren't many killers in Coventry at one time... In fact, I would have said the most likely place a mundane would look would be our family crypt."

"Or the cemetery across from Hangman's House, but woe unto the person that tried to dig up bones from there," I added.

"Yeah, but those witches were murdered. So I don't blame them for being a bit testy."

"And most of them probably never actually killed anybody," I said and tried not to think of our ancestors swinging by their necks from the tree out in front of Hangman's House. "They were just cunning women trying to heal. For the most part."

"Not like us," Lilith said with a laugh and rattled her bag again.

"Hey, now. I try to put murders away. I'm out here right now looking for evidence so we can get one off the street."

"And you're no fun," Lilith said. "Okay, sorry. So I don't do blood rituals. I love my shadow work, but anything involving actual gore is a step outside of my comfort zone. But for a blood ritual, I think you'd want the bones of an executed murderer. Regular old bones of a killer wouldn't be potent enough. If you take our family and the ancestors out of the equation, there are only a few graves."

"We should go check them," I said.

"Well, at least one of them, I harvested dirt from tonight."

"What?"

"Well, I don't use the bones, but the dirt from a grave of an executed murderer is potent stuff. The grave where I performed the ritual tonight was undisturbed. I mean, until I came along."

"What about the others?"

"I rotate which graves I use, so I know where they all are. Come on, let's go check it out."

"Lead the way," I said, and she did.

Kinsley

"So, there was nothing?" I asked.

"No," Mom answered. "Lilith was there collecting graveyard dirt, and she led me on a tour of all of graves. None of them have been exhumed lately."

"Well, then where could he have gotten them from?" It was a rhetorical question.

But Mom answered anyway, "Maybe the internet?"

"You think he ordered the bones of an executed murderer from the internet?"

"Do you have any other ideas?"

"No. But thanks, Mom."

"Not a problem. Hanging out with Lilith and taking a tour of the graveyard is always fun," she said and she meant it. "What are you going to do now?"

"Break into Torin's house and see if he ordered the bones off the internet. If he did, there would probably be a trail on his computer," I said, and I was mostly joking.

"What about the girls?" Mom asked.

"Asleep. We did as much as we could on the history project thing, but they needed to go to bed."

"So, I'll meet you at this Torin person's house in about ten minutes?" she asked.

"You're serious?"

"As death."

"Okay, I'll text you the address," I said, and I did.

I didn't want to lie to Thorn about where I was going, so as I walked from the kitchen, where I'd been on the phone with Mom, into the living room, I tried to prepare my case. I needed to solve the murder, and he could not stand in my way. He'd have to trust me. This thing was outside of human jurisdiction, so breaking and entering wasn't his concern... in this case...

But all of the mental gymnastics I did in preparing for our discussion were a moot point. I walked into the living room and found him asleep on the sofa. "Thorn," I said just to make sure he was really out. He was. Exhausted and dead to the world.

I almost felt bad for sneaking out, but what could I do? I wasn't going to wake him up just to argue about something I was going to do anyway.

So, I grabbed my shoes and purse and headed for the back door. I slipped my shoes on outside and then closed the door as quiet as a whisper.

As I was pulling out of the driveway, I kept expecting to see Thorn appear in the front window or on the porch. He did not, but I was down the street and around the corner before I let out the breath I'd been holding.

When I got to Torin's house, Mom's car was parked down the street. As soon as I pulled in behind her, she and Meri got out on the driver's side.

Since Torin was a bit of a celebrity, he'd chosen a house without any neighbors around. In was in a section of Coventry where there was about one house every two blocks. And no one lived across the street from him. Some of the old houses in the neighborhood had been passed down, through inheritance, to generations that didn't want them. The grand old houses had fallen into disrepair and eventually been razed.

I shuddered to think that the same thing might have happened to Hangman's House if I hadn't returned. Surely, someone else in the coven would have taken care of it, but how could I know that for sure?

"Doesn't look like anyone's around," Mom said.

There was no one outside, and the couple of houses that we could see from Torin's block were completely dark.

"Probably at the festival," I mused. "This neighborhood is mostly old-money witches. Except for Torin."

"Well, let's get inside just in case."

The house was surrounded by a stone wall with an iron gate. The gate lock was rusted through, though, so we easily pushed it open and made our way up the stone walkways to the house's wraparound front porch.

"Think the front door will be as easy as the gate?" Mom asked.

"He didn't seem to concerned with security, but I guess I wouldn't be either if I was an ancient vampire."

"Kind of makes you wonder how they managed to kill him, doesn't it?" Mom asked as I pushed the front door open. She was right, it wasn't locked either.

A shudder passed down my spine. "These are no ordinary witches, but neither are we." While it was true, the words offered me little comfort as we stepped into Torin's dark entryway.

"I'm not scared. I just don't understand it," Mom answered.

"I don't either," I admitted. "But let's find his office. Maybe that will shed some light on this case."

"In here," Meri called from somewhere on the first floor. He'd run ahead and had apparently already found the office.

"In where?" I called back.

"Past the kitchen," Meri answered. "Down the hall on your left. Do I need to draw you a map?"

"No."

We were already on the move when he snarked out the last part. As we got closer, it was easier to tell where he was.

The house was dreadfully dark, and we couldn't turn on any lights. I was even afraid to use the flashlight on my phone because I didn't want to draw attention if someone did happen to walk by the house on an evening stroll.

If not for the bright moonlight, and the fact that some of the curtains were left open, we would've been stumbling around in the dark. As it was, we managed to find a large office with a huge mahogany desk in the middle.

There was a closed laptop on the desk's surface, and next to it was Meri. He swished his tail proudly.

"This doesn't look like somewhere he'd make videos," Mom observed as I sat down at the desk.

"No, but I'm guessing as famous as he was, he had a separate computer for doing the video thing and for personal use." I opened the laptop. "It's password protected."

"Let me," Meri said.

I watched as he tapped a few of the keys with his right paw. "I guess it's a good thing you're a hacker too."

"Not only that, but I'm an excellent researcher too," Meri said as he brought up the web browser and began searching through Torin's internet history.

"I could do that," I said.

"You should keep a lookout," Meri retorted.

"I think that's what Mom is doing," I said when I looked around and realized she wasn't with us.

But just as Meri was about to say something smug, Mom came rushing into the room, but she was bent over. At first, I thought she was hurt or sick. Then, I heard a noise outside and realized she was bent over trying to avoid the windows.

I quickly dropped down to a crouch and Meri jumped off the table. When I heard someone coming through the front door, my instincts kicked in. I didn't know if Meri had found what we were looking for, and we weren't going to be able to search the house further, so I closed the laptop and slipped it into my bag.

Mom rushed past me and signaled for us to follow her. She was heading away from the sound of someone coming through the front entryway, so I followed without question.

It was then I realized that while Meri and I had been messing around with the computer, Mom had been looking around the first floor of the house. She knew the layout of the first floor well enough to lead us to a mudroom with the back door.

We hurried out into the night and scurried around the side of the house. Fortunately for me, the person who had just walked into Torin's place after us hadn't felt the need to hide.

I got a good look at her when she walked by one of the many windows. To my surprise, it was Odessa, the woman who had allegedly broken up with Torin long before his murder. She'd said that she wanted nothing to do with him and just wanted to move on with her life.

So, what was she doing in his house?

Chapter Fifteen

The next morning I was getting ready for the festival, I really needed to go back and check on things, when Chalfy, my manager at Craft Donuts, called and said he had a family emergency. If I wanted Craft Donuts to stay open, I needed to get over there.

I called Mom and she was at my house in less than ten minutes. We said our quick goodbyes, and I left to go relieve Chalfy. He was practically walking out of Craft Donuts as I walked in.

"I'm so sorry, Kinsley. It's my grandpa," he said as he paused for a moment.

I gave him a quick hug because he was like family to me. "Let me know if you need anything," I said as we parted.

He nodded and headed out the door. We were busy as people stopped in for their morning coffee and donut on the way to work. If I didn't have my magic, I probably wouldn't have been able to keep up.

Fortunately, after I'd been there for about an hour, Anise showed up. "Bergamot's going to be late," she said sheepishly. "She had a little too much fun at the festival last night. I told her to go to bed."

I let out a sigh. "I really need to go too."

"Are you going to fire her?" Anise looked stricken.

"For calling in sick once? No. This is just really inconvenient timing."

"She'll be in," Anise said quickly. "I'm going to text her and tell her to get her butt here as soon as she can."

"I appreciate it," I said. "And I'm sorry that I've been out of the loop, but do you know what's going on with Chalfy's grandfather? He hurried out of here so fast, I couldn't get any details."

"He's very sick, and I guess they have to do surgery this morning. Apparently, everyone thought it was going to be fine and his grandfather would come through the surgery with flying colors, but they had some problems with his blood pressure overnight. Chalfy was still going to wait and see him after work, but they downgraded the chances to fifty-fifty," Anise said gravely.

"And he needs to see him before he goes into surgery just in case," I practically whispered.

"But, he has the world's greatest boss, so at least he will get to see him," Anise answered.

"I just wish there was more I could do. If I'd gotten here before he had to run out..."

"We've got him covered. Don't worry, boss," Anise reassured. "All he had to do was get there before the surgery, and he will. All because you will do anything for us."

"I just hope it's enough," I said, but I wasn't sure if I was even just talking about my employees anymore.

I felt pulled in so many different directions. But just as I was starting to relax and fall into the groove of working at the shop, my mom and Laney walked in.

"Hey, guys," I said happy to see them even as a pit formed in my stomach. The kind of pit only a school history fair project can summon...

"We just thought we'd stop in and let you know that we're going shopping for the last few things Laney needs for her project," Mom said.

"Hekate's at school, though?"

"Yeah. Laney's teacher gave them an option day because of the festival. They could attend school today, go to the festival with family, or work on their project if they need it," Mom said.

"But you still need to take Lilith to the festival. She's so looking forward to it," I said.

Just then, Bergamot hurried through the door with her head down. Thirty seconds later, she emerged from the back ready to work.

"Sorry, boss," she mumbled sheepishly. "Won't ever happen again."

"Thanks for coming in," I said and turned back to my mom. "I'll take Laney. The morning rush is over, so Bergamot and Anise can handle the shop."

As Laney looked up at me with total hope and relief, a thought niggled at the back of my mind. Had she done all of this to get my attention? Had I gone too far in my embrace of magic and coven business and let my family duties slip?

"You sure?" Mom asked, but I could tell she was relieved too.

Probably because if she had to cancel on Lilith, my Great-Aunt would have burned the school down in protest. *What is this business about not using magic?* I could hear Lilith's protests as the flames licked the sky.

"I'll take her. You and Lilith have fun. I'm sure Laney and I will have a good time too…"

"All right," Mom agreed as she hugged us goodbye.

"It's not going to be fun, Mom. This project sucks. I don't know why my school decided we had to do it like the regular schoolkids. We're not like them," Laney said as we walked out of the shop into the bright mid-morning sun.

"I don't know, sweetie. I'm sure it will build character, though. Or something like that. We'll do our best to make it fun, and if we can't, just remember not to put things like this off again."

"I'm sorry, Mom."

"You don't need to be sorry, sweetie," I said as we got into the car. "It's just that you don't need to do stuff like this to get my attention, okay? You can just tell me if you need me around more."

Laney looked horrified. "I didn't…" She trailed off as realized dawned on her. "I didn't mean to be bad to get your attention. That's something other kids do. I'm not like that."

"I know," I said with a wink and started the car. "Let's put all this heaviness behind us and try to have some fun at the craft store. Is there any room for glitter in this project?"

I knew that would cheer her up. "No!" she said with a hearty laugh. "I mean, maybe…"

"Well, if it can be done, we'll do it."

The craft store wasn't very busy. There were a couple of other kids from Laney's class there with their parents. The other adults and I exchanged knowing looks. The kids talked for a few minutes about their projects, but everybody knew they needed to stay focused.

Laney and I got some more felt and wooden sticks. She wanted a particular shade of burgundy felt to make a little dress for one of her cut-out people, and one of the craft store employees had to run to the back to see if they had any in stock.

When she emerged from the stockroom holding the last package of burgundy felt, Laney practically squealed with excitement. As it turned out, we were able to make our outing at least a little bit fun.

Once we had everything we needed, Laney and I headed over to the glitter aisle. She might not need it, but you could always use a little more glitter in your life.

Plus, I knew if nothing else, Hekate could smuggle it over to Lilith's house. The two of them liked to make glitter bombs for their enemies. They thought I didn't know about it.

While Laney was deciding between big flakes of purple or pink micro glitter, I happened to hear a conversation in the next aisle over. The voices had been fairly muffled, but I moved closer when I heard my name.

"You know, she's just doing a terrible job at… well, everything," the other woman said once my name had been mentioned.

"I know, right. I heard her kid is in danger of failing the third grade. She's had so many problems with her coven over the years. Remember that time those young witches tried to throw her over? And she had to banish people. Some of those mamas still haven't gotten over their daughters having to leave."

"Why didn't they move too?" the other woman asked earnestly.

"Not the point," she snapped. "Anyway, this festival is a disaster. Of course there would be a murder to ruin everything with her in charge. She seems to attract it. It's almost like she wants these things to happen. Something to distract her from her boring store and stupid donuts."

"I don't know…," the other one hesitated. "But I do think it's a little strange that her friend, who isn't even a real witch, won that pageant. After all those real witches tried so hard. The whole thing was probably rigged for her friend."

"Exactly! And can you believe she didn't even interview those witches with the food stalls next to the murder scene. So much for her crack investigation skills. She just had all of those witches and her fake beauty queen friend move their stuff to other stalls. What if there was evidence in those boxes?"

I felt a tug on my hand. When I looked down, I saw Laney looking up at me with eyes like saucers.

"I heard," Laney said before I could say anything.

"But I..."

"It's okay, Mom. It's still early. We can still get the project done later this afternoon or tonight. We'll have Dad to help us after he gets off work."

"It's just..."

"I know. You have to go talk to those witches. I heard."

"I shouldn't," I said.

"Yes, you should. We'll do it together. We'll do your project first, and then we'll do mine."

Chapter Sixteen

I parked the car right by the entrance to the festival instead of wasting time driving back to the VIP area. The witch directing traffic into parking spots looked like she was going to say something until she saw it was me.

I tossed her my keys. "If it needs to be moved, can you take care of it?" I asked.

"Of course, Kinsley. Yes, ma'am."

"You don't have to call me ma'am," I said over my shoulder.

I took Laney's hand and we marched through the food area until we got to where Torin's body was discovered. Sure enough, the two witches who'd originally contracted to have their food stalls in that location had moved back.

One of them was selling deep-fried desserts. Stuff like deep-fried cheesecake and batter-dipped and fried candy bars. I couldn't be ashamed to admit that once I was done interrogating her, I planned to order one of everything on the menu.

The stall next to her sold pork tenderloin sandwiches. The fried tenderloin fritters were as big as a dinner plate, but they were still stuck on a regular-size bun. They came standard with mustard and pickles, but you could add extra condiments. I planned to get two. For me. Plus, if Laney wanted one.

I had to focus, though. I walked up to the Debbie Does Desserts stall, and the woman, who I presumed was Debbie, turned her attention to us. "Be just a second..." she started to say until she realized it was me. "Oh, Kinsley Wilson. Hello... there... uh... oh... okay... what can I get for you?" she asked when she finally pulled herself together.

"I'm sorry that I haven't been by sooner. I really should have talked to you and the pork tenderloin stall first," I began. "What I need to know is what you saw when Torin was killed. Because it happened right by your stall."

"Kinsley, I would have come to you if I knew anything. I just figured you hadn't come to talk to me because you knew that," she said, and then I realized who she was.

Jasmine had been a friend of the family for a long time. She was much closer to my mother and some of the Aunties, but I knew who she was.

"But did you see or hear anything? Did you have any customers who might have? Maybe I can talk to them."

"My fryer was on the fritz. I showed up right around the time that your friend was having everybody move things. I couldn't start selling treats until I got the fryer fixed," Jasmine said.

"Oh, okay. I mean, can anyone confirm that?"

"Your friend the beauty queen can," Jasmine said, and there was a definite edge to her tone when she said *beauty queen*. "She saw me walk up to the stall holding parts of my fryer and she can tell you no one was there until I got there."

I thought about calling her out on her snide tone about Reggie winning the pageant, but it wasn't the time or the place. I knew people would have a problem with it, and I let it happen anyway.

For a few moments, I contemplated my next move. I could call Reggie and confirm Jasmine's alibi, or I could ask her who repaired her fryer. They would be able to confirm as well. But my family knew her well. Why would she lie to me? I knew where she lived. And more importantly, why would she come back to the festival and keep selling deep-fried candy bars knowing I was looking for the killer?

"Thanks," I finally said. "I appreciate your candor."

"Now, what can I get for you, Kinsley? I know you're not going to leave here without some of these delicious treats."

"I want a deep-fried caramel bar," Laney piped up.

"Anything else?" I turned and asked her. "I was thinking of getting one of everything."

Laney chuckled. "Just the caramel bar, oh, and maybe the deep-fried key lime pie."

"You heard the lady," I said to Jasmine. "One of everything plus an extra caramel bar and slice of the fried key lime pie.'"

"You got it, ma'am," Jasmine said. "That will take a few minutes."

"Okay, well, while you make the food, I'm going to go have this same conversation with the pork tenderloin lady."

"Gillian Krauss," Jasmine said. "That's who's doing the pork Ts. Just come back when you're done, and I'll have everything ready."

"Thanks," I said and took Laney's hand again.

We walked the few feet over to the next stall where Gillian was passing two sandwiches through the window to a couple of expectant customers. She saw me coming and plastered a huge smile on her face.

"How many sandwiches can I get for you ladies?" Gillian asked. My reputation for loving food proceeded me.

"I'll have two. How about you, Laney?"

Laney turned around and looked at the couple who'd just gotten their sandwiches. They'd sat down at a picnic table and dug in.

"I don't know..."

"Oh, they're really good. You'll love them," I said. "Maybe with ketchup and mayo instead of the pickles and mustard, though."

"I'll try it," she answered cheerfully.

"I'll take three sandwiches, and hopefully some information," I said.

"Oh," Gillian's face fell, and I had to wonder what that meant. "I guess I should have figured you were eventually going to ask about that."

"Yeah, and I guess I'm a little disappointed that I did have to ask about it," I admitted. "If you have information, then you really should have come to me."

"That's the thing, Kinsley. I don't. There was that tent between the food stalls, and while that's a little weird, it's not that weird. Not at a festival full of witches. We're all a little mad here."

"So there's nothing. You were here working, but you didn't see anything. No one was ordering pork tenderloins for breakfast, I guess…"

"That's the thing. I was in the back. When I went into the back, the tent was there. When I came back out to help customers, the tent was gone. And, well, you know what they found… It's all because of that dang raccoon. He just happened to be in the back of my stall stealing food when the big reveal happened. It was the darndest thing."

"Yeah, it really was," I said as a lightbulb went off in my head.

Right on time, my Mom and Lilith wandered up. "Hey guys, what are you up to?" Mom asked.

"Oh, hey, Mom. I need to go talk to a witch about a raccoon. I've ordered three pork tenderloin sandwiches and everything on the menu at the Debbie Does Desserts. You, Lilith, and Laney can have it all if you'll watch her for a little while."

"Of course we will, but you don't have to give us all of your food," Mom said.

"Hey, don't speak for me," Lilith retorted. "Better hurry, Kinsley, or it will all be gone."

"Thanks, guys," I said and hurried off toward the VIP section and a particular potion dealer with a wayward raccoon.

Canary Blackwell looked more than a little startled when I barged into her tent. I heard the scurry of tiny paws as her familiar scuttled over the temporary wood floor into the back.

"Kinsley, hi. How can I help you?"

"I just don't know how you did it," I said. "I mean, I suppose you could have doctored the security footage, but I thought I would have picked up on that. I guess I should have known that a witch that adept at glamours could fool me."

"I have no idea what you're talking about," Canary said.

"Your familiar. She was in the back of the pork tenderloin stall distracting the proprietor during the ritual and after."

"She steals food all of the time," Canary protested, but her face turned white as a sheet. "She must have..."

"It could have been a coincidence, but I saw her again. I just didn't realize it at the time. She was at a house where the victim and the killer were hiding stolen books. Books I assume they were using for the blood ritual. I saw her there, but at the time, I didn't recognize her. She had the good sense to be out without her tutu. But, thinking back, I know it was her."

"LULU!" Canary shrieked, but she seemed genuinely shocked and angry.

While we waited for the trash panda to come forward and face the music, I tried to put the pieces together in my mind. Lulu seemed to be the clue that held it all together, but how?

"Kinsley, I swear I don't know what's going on. Please tell me what she's done," Canary pleaded.

"I'm not entirely sure," I said and bit my bottom lip in frustration. "I can tie Lulu, the cigarettes, and Torin's ex-girlfriend together with the house. I found his cigarettes there, and those turned out to be Odessa's, but she has an alibi too. I saw her on video during the murder, and that doesn't even take into account the vampire that attacked us at the library."

"A vampire attacked you at the library? And that has something to do with Lulu? I'm so confused," Canary said. "LULU!" she yelled again.

"You didn't see it," Meri said as he sauntered into the tent.

"What?" I asked. "What are you saying?"

"You didn't go back and look at the security footage at Scoops of Fun. Odessa told you that Gladys would confirm her story. You didn't look at the footage or ask Gladys because you just assumed she couldn't pull off a lie like that."

"And she couldn't," I said. "Unless she was sure Gladys would confirm her story."

"Or she was sure you wouldn't ask," Meri groused. "Because you're too easy. Brighton never would have just let it go like that."

"I'm not my mother…" I had to admit he was right. My mother was a different kind of witch. She never would have just let Odessa's story go like that.

"Tell me about it," Meri snarked.

"LULU!" Canary yelled again, and then she started for the back.

"Oh, no. You wait here," I said as I straightened my back. I could be hardcore.

"I need to go see what she's up to," Canary said.

255

"Meri, you go. And drag that raccoon up here kicking and screaming if you have to. She has answers, and I want them."

"That's the spirit," Meri said, and I could have sworn he looked proud.

"He's not going to hurt her, is he?" Canary wrung her hands in front of her.

"Not unless she's a demon," I said offhand.

"She's not," Canary blanched. "I don't know what she's gotten herself into this time, but she's not evil."

"You seem to be making a lot of excuses," I said. "And what do you mean, this time?"

"She just... I know she steals food, but she's a raccoon."

"That's it? She steals food?"

"No," Canary finally admitted. "I think she's stolen potions and ingredients from me before."

"What kind of potions and ingredients?" I asked.

"It doesn't matter. Just a little bit of everything. The why she's doing it is what's important. I think she sells them... probably to buy food."

"So, you're saying you think Lulu stole some of your potions or ingredients to help the witches kill Torin?"

"If she did, she didn't do it to help kill him. Lulu isn't evil. She's just... not very bright," Canary said with a sigh.

"Then why is she hiding from me?"

"Honestly, you're kind of scary when you're mad, Kinsley. Also, she knows the witches she helped killed him. She had to have known if you figured it out, she'd be in trouble."

"That's putting it lightly," I said. "I need to see her. If she won't come out, then I need to go in the back and get her. Canary, I don't believe you're involved in this, so please don't get in my way."

She hung her head. "I know. Just please don't kill her."

"I'm not sure what her punishment will be, but right now, I just want to talk to her. I'm not going to kill her."

"Thank you," Canary said and then stepped aside.

But when I went into the back, Meri was getting ready to leave the tent through the back. "I looked everywhere back here, but I'm pretty sure the raccoon did a runner as soon as we arrived."

"I'm not surprised," I said with a sigh.

Just then, my phone rang. Normally, I'd ignore it when I was so deep in such an important investigation. But knowing it could be about the girls, I had to look.

Instead, I saw that it was Thorn. "What's up, sweetie? I'm real close to nailing this murder down, so I don't have much time to talk. I have to hunt down a wayward raccoon familiar."

"I don't think you do," he said. "I had a deputy nearby, so he's already at Scoops of Fun, and I'm on my way right now."

"What happened?" For a terrible moment, I was afraid the case was about to get a lot more complex. Turned out to be the opposite.

"Nothing happened, per se. It's the darndest thing. A woman called from the shop and said that she and her employee wanted to confess to the recent murder. They said that their only condition was for us to come take them to jail right away."

"You don't think it's some kind of trick?"

"Nope. When the deputy arrived, they had written confessions signed and ready for us. He's got them handcuffed and waiting in the back of his cruiser. I'm just going to take a quick look at everything, and then we're taking them to jail."

When we hung up, I turned back to Canary. "I believe Odessa and Gladys confessed so that they'd get thrown in the human jail. I need to speak to the vampires and make sure they don't attack trying to get to them. I'll deal with Lulu later. I'm pretty sure she went and warned them, and right now I don't know if she saved me a massive headache or created a new one."

Epilogue

So, it turned out that the royal vamps were so disgusted with Torin for "consorting with filthy witches" that they viewed his death as a favor. With friends like that...

Odessa and Gladys had confessed to the murders long before it got out that the vampires weren't going to exact vengeance, so they went to prison anyway. I was never going to live it down with Thorn that in the end, it was human justice that prevailed. So I let him have the victory. He strutted around for a couple of days with his chest puffed out because he felt like a manly man, and I made his favorite dinner. His life was on the line, after all. The vampire conclave could have ambushed him or the sheriff's station to get to the killers. Thankfully, they didn't.

At the end of the day, all-out war between witches and vampires was avoided. Oh, and Coventry got a new potions master. I agreed to let Lulu live, but only if she was indentured to my coven for a thousand years. Canary didn't want to abandon her, so she stayed in Coventry.

Lilith has already taken a liking to the conniving little raccoon. I know, it's totally shocking...

As to why Odessa and Gladys wanted Torin's blood, and why they killed him, and also why Torin went along with any of it, the answers are vanity and obsession.

Torin couldn't stand that Odessa had left him, and he was willing to do anything to get her back. So he agreed to partake in a blood ritual when Odessa said that she would love him again.

As to the purpose of the blood ritual, that's where the vanity comes into play. Gladys wanted to be young again. Or at the very least, she wanted to look young again. She was a bad witch, but she managed to steal enough information to cobble together a ritual and potion recipe to turn back the clock.

Except that again, she was a bad witch, and the ritual killed Torin. Even with the help of the ley line and the festival's massive magical energy, they couldn't pull it off.

And Odessa was just involved because she wanted to help Gladys. You see, the older woman wasn't just an employee. She was

Odessa's adoptive mother. Oh, and she was a raging manipulative narcissist too.

Apparently, getting arrested and going to prison was enough to break Gladys' thrall over Odessa. I'd heard that Odessa requested that she be put in a different prison, as far away from Gladys as possible. Since she confessed, the judge granted her request.

She was probably free for the first time in her life. But it wasn't necessary for her to get assigned to a separate prison, because Gladys never made it to hers.

Her prison transport was ambushed, and while none of the guards were hurt, Gladys disappeared without a trace. But don't worry, she's safe and secure in the Skeenbauer family crypt. While she's not family, we consider her an enrichment activity for all of the souls trapped in there. We couldn't leave a witch, even a terrible one, out there to create more havoc. And prisons are full of broken women she could've easily manipulated. It was a risk no one in the coven was willing to take.

But onto the most important conflict resolution in this story, Laney's history fair project. I skipped the rest of the Beltane Festival to help her finish it.

She got an A-. I was proud of us, but when all was said and done, I still gave her a month's chores with no magic use. I figured a month of doing dishes and sweeping floors without being able to use magic would bring the point home. She didn't complain too much. Although, I did suspect that Bonkers was giving her a little magical assistance. But what could I do? That's what familiars are for.

Thank you for reading!

Made in United States
North Haven, CT
23 August 2022

23084559R00147